RENCOR
LIFE IN GRUDGE CITY

RENCOR
LIFE IN GRUDGE CITY

MATT WALLACE

FROM A STORY BY
KEITH J. RAINVILLE
AND
MATT WALLACE

ILLUSTRATIONS BY
JESSE JUSTICE

FROM PARTS UNKNOWN
Los Angeles, California

Rencor: Life in Grudge City
by
Matt Wallace

from a story by
Keith J. Rainville
and
Matt Wallace

Print Edition

©2016 Matt Wallace and Keith J. Rainville

ISBN #978-0-9753791-7-2

Original illustrations © Jesse Justice, 2015
Cover design by Keith J. Rainville/FPU

From Parts Unknown Publications
2658 Griffith Park Boulevard #163
Los Angeles, California 90039
www.FromPartsUnknown.com

www.Matt-Wallace.com

El Mil Calaveras III
Estilo: RUDO

El Victor III
Estilo: TÉCNICO

PROLOGUE: MIDNIGHT

Drawing the blinds of his office in Rencor Police Department Headquarters, Captain Gustavo Bustamante drops the plastic container of salad inside the bottom drawer of his desk and slams it shut. He hides it there instead of at the bottom of his trashcan so not even the janitor will discover it. Gus doesn't trust the old bastard not to gossip with the members of his squad.

He opens his top desk drawer, reaching far in the back and removing a bag of mini BuBu Lubus. He rips through several wrappers in succession, shoving their classic strawberry, marshmallow, and chocolate candy contents in his mouth the way a chain smoker inhales multiple cigarettes on their coffee break.

Gus ordered that salad for lunch in good faith.

He really did.

It is today's fault, not his, that it will go uneaten.

As he stuffs his fifth BuBu Lubu in his mouth, Gus reflects with malice upon the fact that every cop reacts to stress differently. You'd never catch him drinking himself into a stupor, or downing pills, or inhaling noxious smoke, or going home and beating his wife and kids. Yet none of those far more harmful activities have earned any of his colleagues such a hated nickname within the department.

"Gus the Bus."

That's what they call him behind his back.

He's only heard it out loud once, and Gus crammed the head that spoke those words inside a locker filled with soiled workout sweats. It hasn't stopped the other cops from using it, however. He can always tell.

Gus's weight simply is what it is. He hasn't been below two hundred and fifty pounds since he was a teenager, and he was never that tall to begin with. It's only slowed him down in recent years, and he's supposed to be an administrator now, anyway. Gus is and has always been a good cop who works hard. He's just a hopelessly emotional eater.

Gus is stressed to the point of chocolate today because Medianoche, the old enmascarado hero, is waiting outside his office.

It's Gus's job to fire him.

The task is bad enough, but Gus isn't just firing one man, he's effectively ending an entire era of heroism with one sentence.

When Gus was coming up, back when he wore a uniform and walked a beat, there was never an official term within the department for the luchadores who "helped" the police solve crimes and combat citywide threats. They weren't just part of the culture and the landscape of Rencor, they were woven into its very fabric. They were, in the reality of the border city, what purely American superheroes could only be in comic books.

But then attendance at the arena began dropping off.

Gradually, the media and the city council and the public at large all began to realize they were uncomfortable with masked luchadores running around the city fighting bandits and mad scientists. They even started blaming the enmascarados for the latter. The dreaded words "masked vigilante" were spoken more than once.

It was a dangerous path, and one that needed to be headed off.

So the enmascadaro-as-crimefighter officially became the "Rencor PD Auxiliary Patrol." The enmascarados willing to stay on had their powers and authority clearly defined and greatly limited from what they'd been before. It effectively ended the era of lucha-heroes doing battle on rooftops, kicking in doors, and pursuing crooks who themselves were equally over-the-top.

Basically they were allowed to investigate, but were required to call in the "real" cops to do the rest.

That placated everyone for a while.

Gus was a lieutenant with an eye on his captain stripes when the final shift occurred.

Crime in Rencor had changed along with everything else in the world, it seemed. Gone were the days of werewolves and zombie sightings reported near cemeteries and recounted seriously in all the papers. Gone were the hooded rudos, the villainous luchadores with grand schemes of taking over the city that always ended in their técnico rivals standing triumphantly over their pummeled forms and never-fired death rays.

All of those things faded into memory.

Worse than that, they faded into novelty, taking the enmascarado with them.

Now deadly street gangs infested Rencor, doing the bidding of even more lethal cartels. Drive-by killings in the streets. Serial murderers with no grand Machiavellian world-domination schemes, only dreams of perverse, terrifying carnage.

Crime became a truly ugly, vile, infectious thing, beyond the purview of masked heroes.

The Rencor PD Auxiliary Patrol was disbanded.

The era of the luchador crimefighter was finally over.

Gus's predecessor managed to keep a number of the old-timer enmascarados on the payroll, the ones who weren't in shape to go back on the road as wrestlers and who the city owed a great debt, even if most in it had forgotten. They officially became "consultants," advising the force on relevant matters if and when they occurred.

But, of course, a younger generation was leading the charge in the police department now, and most of them didn't want to hear from old men in colorful masks about anything, let alone fighting "real" criminals in the so-called "real world."

The ranks of the enmascarado consultants shrunk, some retiring their hoods altogether, others claimed by old age, until the department finally decided to shutter the position completely.

The last lucha-heroes who remained were relegated to touring schools, giving say-no-to-drugs-and-bad-guys speeches, glad-handing at policeman's balls and bake sales and the like.

Most were happy to still be relevant in that way.

Medianoche refused all of these offers.

He was a crimefighter.

And now he's the last of the crimefighters.

It takes half the bag of BuBu Lubus and an entire bottle of pineapple Jarritos soda pop before Gus is ready to call him in.

He presses the buzzer on his desk, and a moment later the aging hero ambles in, smiling openly beneath his orange hood with its iconic hourglass symbol emblazoned on the forehead. Medianoche was a physical beast in his prime, but pushing seventy he's become a round, pudgy man from head to toe.

"Hola, Capitán," the five-time champion greets him.

Gus stands briefly and motions to one of the empty chairs on the other side of his desk.

"Have a seat, my friend."

Medianoche squeezes himself between the arms of a chair.

"Did I ever tell you," Gus begins tentatively, retaking his own seat, "you wrestled in the first match I ever saw?"

Medianoche shakes his head.

"Against Super Reactor Three," Gus continues, a wistful smile coming to his face at the memory. "You dove out of the ring right onto him, right in front of me and my tío. It was...amazing. You were amazing."

"I haven't done that dive in a long time," is all Medianoche says.

Gus nods. "It was the same dive you used to take out those bank robbers back in...whenever it was. It was my first week on the force, though. I remember that. An all-cars call went out for Banco de Rencor. We surrounded the building. Man, they charged out those front doors, three of them, armed to the teeth. They were wearing those big parrot heads, like they were in a parade. I froze. I did. A lot of us did. But they never got a shot off. You came diving off the big cement awning over the doors of the damn bank right on top of them, flattened all three."

Medianoche nods, grinning wide and genuinely as his own recall kicks in.

"What did you yell?" Gus asks.

"You know what I yelled," the enmascarado chides him. "Everyone back then knew what I yelled."

"C'mon," Gus pleads. "One more time. Please. For me."

Medianoche sighs, then, body tensing in his chair and fists raised, lets out a powerful yell of, "Time's up, cabrones!"

Gus explodes into joyous laughter.

Medianoche soon joins him.

It lasts as long as it can, until they both remember why they're here, and that the days of Medianoche yelling out catchphrases as he topples bad guys have long past.

Fading laughter is one of the world's worst sounds.

"I owe you a lot, man," Gus says after it has died out. "The whole city owes you a lot. And I just...I want to tell you—"

Medianoche waves a heavy hand, silencing him.

"All those debts have been paid," Medianoche assures him, sincerely. "I made my money. I got my props, the cheers of the crowd. For years I had that. No one owes me nothing, especially not you."

Medianoche stands, slowly, his every joint cracking audibly as he does.

Gus follows suit, standing out of respect, almost ready to salute the man.

Instead he asks him, "What will you do?"

Medianoche shrugs.

Then something happens that Gus will dream about for the rest of his life.

Some of the dreams will be good.

Most of those dreams won't be.

Medianoche's hands, knotted from decades of grappling and scarred from bare-knuckle brawling, reach up and deftly tug apart the laces behind his hood.

With one smooth, silent motion, he removes his mask.

Gus immediately looks away, as if Medianoche is concealing the sun itself beneath his hood. No one outside of their families ever sees an enmascarado's face, not unless they lose their mask in a match. It's as sacred as a priest's robes, and even more mysterious.

Medianoche waits.

Eventually Gus manages to turn his head back to the unmasked hero. Medianoche's face is, of course, wholly unremarkable.

He's just a man now, like any other.

"Maybe I'll rob a bank," Medianoche says with a smile, winking.

He places his legendary mask down upon Gus's desk, gently, and turns to leave the office. He pauses with his hand on the doorknob, looking back at the captain.

"You know," Medianoche says, "I always thought if I was unmasked it'd be in the ring. Time was supposed to be my power. My ally. I never thought of it as my opponent. But it was. It did what no rudo could. It took Medianoche's máscara."

Those are the last words he says to Gus.

He's been gone for several long moments when Captain Bustamante picks up Medianoche's hood. The textile still feels warm and heavy in his hands.

Gus always dreamt of being a cop, protecting people.

He never in his worst nightmares imagined he'd kill one of his childhood heroes.

PART ONE

TÉCNICO

TEN YEARS AGO

You can't see blood under the máscara. Oh, blood can and will create dark spots under lighter colored masks, but the familial men who've worn the hood of El Victor have never had that problem. Their mask has always been blood red cloth with a curved and sharply pointed "V" cut out of leather or vinyl stitched over its face. Their hoods have hidden three generation's worth of viscous head wounds sustained in countless four-cornered professional wrestling and lucha libre rings all around the globe.

It has always been the unofficial family motto: No one should ever see a Victor bleed.

The latest of his line to don the red-and-white hood, El Victor III had to reach the absolute height of his career before he truly understood the double meaning of that phrase.

That height occurred, of course, in Coliseo Rencor, both the geographic center of the city of Rencor and the grudge-settling center of the lucha world. It's the arena that ended more bloody feuds than a loaded shotgun. Every masked wrestling rivalry that mattered fought its final battle inside the towering, dilapidated concrete edifice arched like an Aztec crown.

El Victor had to be helped back to the técnico locker room after the match by his father, Victor II, and his cousin and fellow masked wrestler, El Lágrima Rojo. Both men also wore their masks; his father's the mirror image of Victor's, save for the small Roman numeral "II" on the side, and his cousin's, a black hood with a red teardrop in glittered vinyl under the left eye hole. Rojo always wore a gangster bandana over the forehead of the mask, his gimmick popular with the younger fans even if it went against the classic hero's grain of the rest of the family.

Swaths of blood that weren't his own but nevertheless lathered Victor's torso also stained his father's perfectly tailored double-breasted suit. The suit was a brilliant burgundy, the wide lapels pure white, perfectly mimicking the family's iconic masks. Even his tie was red with a white "V" embroidered at the bottom.

Victor II couldn't have cared any less about ruining the suit he had made specifically in support of his son's match that night. He cradled his triumphant heir with one arm and held the boy's ten-pound gold championship belt in the other, a belt that once belonged to him and was lost and won many times over.

Blood stains were a cheap price to pay.

The cheers of the crowd still filled every corridor, every room, every hidden nook beyond the arena floor, like some potent drug absorbed in the bloodstream and carried through a body's every vein. They were still on their feet fifteen minutes after the end of the match, over twenty thousand fans, in what was already the longest standing ovation in Grudge City history.

Victor no longer heard the chants. For him the world had become muted. He existed in that moment only inside his mask. He felt no physical pain, not even from the deep cuts and bruises and bone stresses throughout his battered body, not even as he limped and had to grip with half-broken hands his father and cousin for strength and balance.

Good guys aren't supposed to throw closed fists in a wrestling match, but most good guys never had to fight a war against Calavera.

Victor's only thought was that it was over. It wasn't the match that was over, or even the feud the match had closed the book upon. No, something much larger than that was over, but Victor couldn't quite define for himself what that was.

He just knew something bigger than any of its parts, however grand, had come to an end.

It dominated his thoughts and shut out the feeling of victory he should've been experiencing.

Victor's internal mute button was shattered as his father and cousin helped him across the threshold of the locker room. The sudden sensory explosion—the flash bulbs of antiquated cameras, the cacophony of the reporters holding them, the popping of a dozen champagne bottle corks, the cheering of the other técnicos — the "good guy" wrestlers — all of it came crashing over him in one jagged wave.

It was still the same locker room in which he'd geared-up a thousand times or more. It was the still the apotheosis of all pro-wrestling locker rooms; the heat of too many bodies in too confined a space, the musky smell of sweat and the heavy, often cheap colognes the workers used to mask it during long loops of shows with limited showers in-between. There was the silent kid in the time-honored "towel boy" mask passed down from young arena intern to young arena intern, pushing a rubber bin of dirty towels.

It was El Victor's home away from home, as it had always been.

Tonight, however, it was filled with rare fireworks. After his victory over El Mil Calaveras III, also know as "The Man of a Thousand Skulls," it was the party to end all parties.

They'd worked each other in the ring over one hundred times in the past five years, but tonight had been different. Tonight had been their last match, the final battle in their longstanding, arena filling, and block-buster feud.

Tonight had been the Loser-Leaves-Town Match.

And El Victor was the victor.

Calavera, his arch-nemesis, himself being carried to the back by his similarly masked family, would have his contract terminated at midnight, and by morning he'd be gone from Ciudad Rencor forever.

He was banished.

Exiled in and by defeat.

They'd never wrestle again.

Victor had won their feud, a three-generations-old feud.

He was a hero.

Actually, he'd already been a hero.

With this victory he'd pass into legend.

Beside him, his father, Victor II, was laughing and clapping his son on the back. It was the first time since the ending bell of the match rang out that Victor felt the pain of his injuries.

¡Sonreír! His brain shouted at him. Smile, cabrón! You're the champ!

The voice inside his head at that moment sounded very much like his father and his grandfather speaking in unison, instructing him in far more than wrestling ever since he could walk.

El Victor smiled through the small vinyl-lined window in the mouth of his mask for the cameras, the reporters, the executives from the front office, and the boys — the other luchadores.

He felt something cold, wet, and foamy raining over his shoulders and down his back, and realized his cousin was pouring a bottle of champagne over him and laughing.

The voice inside his head instructed him to join in the laughter, and so he did, loud and heartily.

Then he became aware of the questions being lobbed at him in almost indistinguishable volleys by the press.

They asked him how he thought that match had gone.

They asked him about his strategy, and how well he thought he'd executed it.

Was he nervous after being pinned by Calavera and losing the first of three falls?

How had he managed to rally after Calavera nailed Victor in the groin with his favored illegal skull brass knuckles while the referees were distracted trying to keep their families from tearing each other apart?

Victor answered each question automatically, as if he'd heard them a thousand times before, and he had.

They asked him a dozen more questions until finally someone threw out the one he'd been dreading.

It was the question Victor absolutely knew how to answer and absolutely did not know how to process.

The press asked him how he felt.

He must've hesitated too long, as his father finally tensed beside him and prodded him for an answer with a subtle but stern shoulder prod.

Victor heard an infectious quiet spread through the raucous space.

Even the voice in his head seemed at a loss.

"I feel like...a Victor!" he finally said, and his words would become the dominant headline tomorrow.

The lights began flashing, the voices raised, and the champagne corks popped anew.

Victor didn't hear any more of their questions.

Masks can and do hide more than blood.

That night, in that moment, Victor's mask hid something else, something he chose to stuff down deep and not acknowledge. But he knew one thing. That feeling would wait there, in that banished place inside him, for as long as it took.

FALLEN IDOLS

The luchador, being the designated muscle of the group, takes the lead. His padded wrestling boots make little sound on the rocky floor of the cave, but the gentle crackle of the flaming torch he carries seems like a cacophony in the tense silence. It's only a matter of time before the sound leads...*it*...right to them. El Victor sheds his Crimson ring jacket in preparation.

The first howl bounces off the cave walls and freezes the trio in their tracks.

Carla, being the daughter of the university's preeminent crypto-zoological expert, knows what's coming and covers her mouth with a gasp, ducking slightly so her tall blonde beehive hairdo doesn't hit the cave ceiling. Getting a confident nod from Victor, she remembers the ancient book of witchcraft she's carrying and quickly flips through its pages to a marked passage, reading it aloud in a shaky voice.

"Father!" Victor summons the holy man with a voice as deep as the hero is strong. "It is time!"

Father Plácido rushes to Victor, takes his torch in one hand and crosses the hero's mask with the other in a frantic blessing. The pure silver metal 'V' that's been fastened over the signature faceplate of Victor's mask gleams in the firelight. Hours ago it was an ornate Spanish cross decorating the mission's altar, now melted down and shaped by the local blacksmith into a blessed piece of facial armor.

The second howl is closer, much closer. Silhouetted by flame, Victor tightens his boots' laces and adjusts his knee pads over his red trunks. He shakes out his arms and clenches his fists, limbering up like he would any night in the squared circle.

This is anything but another night at the Coliseo, however.

The third howl comes from close enough that the sound of rushing footsteps accompanies it, and the luchador half-crouches into a ready stance, weight forward, arms wide, on the balls of his feet. Doing so probably saves his life, for when the creature suddenly appears out of the darkness it is already airborne.

Once a normal man, the thing that plows into Victor's midsection is now bigger, stronger and faster than he is. Its checkered shirt and pants are merely shreds interrupted by long swatches of fur akin to a horse's mane. Its four incisors are now inches longer, bathed in the white froth of rabid rage.

Two swipes of razor-sharp claws leave a grid of blood trails across the masked man's barrel chest. The hero counters with a broad arcing slap of his own, followed by a series of open-handed cross-arm chops to the creature's collarbones and neck. It gives Victor the separation he needs for a perfectly placed two-footed drop kick to the chest, sending his supernatural opponent into the jagged rock wall. The beast screams, as much in frustration as pain.

It charges again, more erratic, but leaves a wildly thrown arm outstretched a second too long. Victor grabs its hairy wrist, fulcrums the elbow with his other arm and falls into a corkscrew motion to the ground. Something snaps loudly and the creature roars and thrashes away with its legs in a panic.

The damage has been done, its right arm hangs broken, dislocated.

The werewolf is disoriented, it has never known this crippled state, this pain, as either man or wolf. It has never encountered a predator that was its equal, has never fought against educated limbs and veteran technique. But in fear, cornered, it gains in ferocity.

The final charge is so wanton, so desperate and anarchic in its violence that it takes Victor's finest reflexes to merely survive. He ducks under onto his back and throws the beast over him with a rolling monkey flip. Even off its feet the wolf swings, its one good claw so dangerously close to slicing the masked man's jugular, Carla screams in panic.

The wolf lands and recovers, turning its head toward the terrified co-ed, distracted for one fatal second.

This time it is Victor who pounces, charging like a rhino, hitting the monster full force in the breadbasket. The spear is an instinctual, fundamental wrestling move Victor doesn't think twice about. However no ring opponent ever reacted to the strike like this.

The creature reels in pain, clutching its abdomen, which is *smoking*.

Father Plácido's eyes widen and he crosses himself, as Victor touches the silver faceplate on his mask with reverence and inspiration.

He seizes the moment, grabbing a handful of knotted hair from the beast's head. Leaning back into a kick like a baseball pitcher, he shoots his head forward into a devastating head-butt.

The fire in the monster's eyes goes dimmer, and Victor strikes again, this time grabbing the beast in a bear-hug, trapping it's arms, delivering a second head-butt at close quarters. The beast wails, the flesh and hair around its forehead starting to singe and smoke. Victor delivers a third strike, and a fourth.

With the impact of the fifth, something gives, and the champion pauses his fury and releases his foe.

Victor's signature V has seared into the creature's head and face. Trails of smoke and the stench of burning hair fill the cave. The man-wolf's eyes go blank, and it drops to the ground.

The priest leans over the dead creature who, as last rights are given, reverts back to the bruja-cursed ranch hand he once was.

Carla runs over to embrace Victor, but he keeps her at a respectable arm's length with an appreciative brace of the shoulders.

After a 'my work here is done' nod, he departs the cave, standing arms akimbo in the light of the full moon.

Violins surge.

The word 'FIN' appears over his chest.

"And the crowd goes wild..." El Victor III muses as the familiar 'Peliculas Rencor' eagle logo fades off the screen.

Applause trickles from the 20 or so people in the El Pachuco Theater, echoing sporadically around walls that have seen better days.

Before the house lights fully come up, Victor darts out of the theater, glad-hands the old usher in the lobby who's known him since before he was masked, and heads out into the street to find his elders.

La Pachuco Theater opened in downtown Rencor at the height of his father's wrestling and film career, and just after his grandfather retired from both. Its owner was another enmascarado with a popular zoot-suiter gimmick, complete with a wide-brimmed feathered hat, fashioned entirely from vinyl, stitched to the top of his mask. His likeness remains in the form of third-scale busts fashioned into the columns on either side of the theater's entrance, though the man himself passed into legend decades ago.

One of Pachuco's final acts was to sign the Victors to an exclusive promotional contract. On the third Saturday of every month, he would showcase a matinee double feature of classic monster movies starring the legendary luchadores – Victor I's being old black-and-white serials, II's more colorful fare from decades later. In-between showings the masked men would sit behind a table signing autographs and taking Polaroids with the fans that turned out for the events.

When Victor III first began accompanying his father and grandfather to the signings they were a big-ticket item every single month. Rabid fans would line up around the block for two seconds of the family's time and a brief handshake. Press attended, snapping pictures to run in the city papers or filming short clips to play at the very end of the evening news. There would be an army of food carts and merchandise vendors bombing through the crowd. Mariachi bands played raucously for the people. Now and again the featured film's monster would turn up in costume for one of them to throw a headlock around to the crowd's immense pleasure.

It was a party worthy of heroes.

That party slowed down somewhat after Victor II's retirement, but when his son, the new El Victor, fully took up the mantle the crowds returned in full. Though the time of the luchador-starring B-monster movie of the week had long since passed, whenever Victor III turned up in a direct-to-video (and direct-to-DVD after it) movie or soap opera, it always received an ultra-limited run at La Pachuco and the party started anew.

When he began his feud with El Mil Calaveras III the crowds exploded, especially on the occasions when Calavera himself turned up to hype one of their upcoming matches and taunt Victor into an impromptu brawl through the theater aisles.

It led to simulcast pay-per-views from the over-sold-out arena filling the Pachuco like never before. The mariachis became rock and roll bands, and odd people calling themselves 'zine publishers' moved among the traditional press, but all in all it was a glorious return to Victor II's heyday.

Unfortunately, as they inevitably do, times changed.

In the ten years since El Victor battled Calavera in their Loser-Leaves-Town match, no other spectacle lived up to that crescendo of a night. At first the crowds waited patiently for the next stars, the next feud, to ascend to that Victor/Calavera plateau.

None did.

Promoters tried, of course. One of the advantages of the almost no-man's-land perception of Rencor and its existence between the US and Mexico both geographically and culturally has always been its freedom from strictly lucha libre traditions. When the Loser-Leaves-Town match was announced, it was revolutionary. The old-timey American concept didn't exist in lucha, and it became a sensation.

Other attempts at popularizing such non-traditional gimmicks were less successful, and their follow-ups outright failures. Japanese death matches, American-style "Money in the Bank" matches. The right balance between foreign influence and old school lucha could never seem to be struck, or perhaps the right enmascarados to bring them off simply no longer existed.

Banishing Calavera had broken attendance records, but it had also left a longer-term hole that no one seemed able to fill.

And without the right villain, no hero is worth the cover price of a comic book.

Ten years didn't used to be that long in Rencor wrestling where feuds spanned generations. But in the internet age ten years became an eternity.

On this particular Saturday at La Pachuco the marquee reads, "EL VICTOR CONTRA EL LOBO DE LA BRUJA" (1955 – Victor I's first film) and "EL VICTOR Y PROFESSOR GORILLA EN BERMUDA" (1987 – Victor II's final film, a not-so-funny comedy).

The two elder Victors dutifully crew their signing table outside the theater.

Grandpa Victor upgraded to an electronic wheelchair several years ago, although he still carries his ornate cane crowned with silver "V" wherever he motors himself. He speaks exclusively in Spanish, largely out of spite and especially around gringo tourists. The single suit he wears was purchased for the premiere of his final movie in the 1960's and never replaced.

His son and grandson think his refusal to unmask, even in the privacy of his own home, is because the near-century-old enmascarado's hands are wracked with constant tremors and unable to undo the laces anymore, and the old man would rather never take his hood off than accept help.

The truth is Grandpa Victor has come to enjoy how repelling people find the smell of the constantly stewing and sun-baked leather hood.

His son is the exact opposite. Still a barrel-chested bear of a man, just a little more grizzled around his increasingly weathered gills, the aging Victor II revels in donning his finest double-breasted suit and oxblood leather shoes every morning, whether or not he's appearing in public. He also made the transition to the ease of a zippered hood in his retirement, and as such his vinyl mask shines in the afternoon sun whereas his father's simply slow-roasts.

"¡Yo quiero ir a casa!" Grandpa Victor protests for the third time in the past hour, slamming his cane against the arms of his motorized chair.

"We have to stay 'til the second movie is done," his son reminds him.

Thus far they've had a bus from the senior citizen home stop by, a few diehard fans of Victor II's, and a couple of border town tourists who obviously didn't know who any of the luchadores are, but took dozens of pictures on their smartphones anyway before moving on to the zebra-painted donkey set up down the street.

There are only a few people milling around the theater entrance when Victor III joins them. His elders make it a point to adjust their ties and lapels as they look down the noses of their masks at his wardrobe — stingray cowboy boots, embroidered jeans, and the *Héroes Cotidianos* logo t-shirt (from his own clothing line, available on his website, of course).

One might think he was ring security in a concession-bought mask if it weren't for the solid gold Rolex (possibly the only one in the city that's not a knock-off) around his wrist and the ornate buckle on his belt — practically as large as an iPad mini and inlaid with pearls and rubies that carry the family V motif.

The third El Victor is more or less in the same fighting shape he was the night of his last match with Calavera. He works out fanatical-ly, especially since increasingly less of his time is taken up by actually touring, wrestling and general hero work. Though the lithe build of his high-flying days is behind him, he still looks trim enough to run a mara-thon, hovering somewhere between that top-flight young wrestler and the filled-out grizzly his father has become.

Victor sips from an energy drink he once endorsed (he has several dozen cases of them stacked in his basement; they did not sell well). The few fans remaining immediately flock around him, thrusting articles for him to sign and clinging to him to snap selfies.

Victor accommodates them with a practiced smile and smooth, equally practiced words.

"I saw your last match at the Coliseo with my tío when I was twelve," a seventeen-year-old kid in thick, horn-rimmed glasses informs him excitedly. "When are you going to wrestle in Rencor again, Victor?"

"I'm enjoying the rest," Vic answers automatically and with a manufactured chuckle, only feeling the sting of the question somewhere deep in the back of his mind. "Besides, I have to give all these young vatos coming up a chance to shine, right? That's what a good champion does."

He breezes past the kid with a pat on the shoulder and steps up to his father and grandfather's table.

"¿Qué tal, mijo?" Victor II greets him with a proud smile.

"Just thought I'd stop by, see how the, uh...signing...was going. You were lookin' good fighting that bruja's wolf boy, Abuelito." He says to his grandfather, getting a mild 'aw shucks' slap across the chest in response.

"Stay for the second feature, it's *really* funny!" his father beams."

"Lo siento, I gotta go..."

"Where are you off to today?"

"El Barón called. He wants to see me at the Coliseo."

"¡Chingón!" Victor's grandfather hisses, spitting over the side of his motorized chair in open disdain.

The vinyl above Victor II's eyes crinkles as he furrows his brow. "Does he finally want to put you back at the top of the card?"

"He didn't say."

"Well, if it's not that, then you don't have anything to discuss with that man. He's greedier than his father ever was, and he has no respect for the past, or the workers who built what he has now."

Victor is nodding impatiently halfway through his father's gentle tirade. "I know all of that. I'm still running a business, Pop. If he wants a meeting, then I meet with him. But I know. I promise."

"I trust you, mijo. You know how to handle yourself like a Victor. Just keep on your toes when you talk to that...that..."

"¡Chingón!" Grandpa repeats, spitting again.

"Sí, Tito, sí," Victor says, placating the old man.

Victor glances up and down the mostly deserted street. The buildings are dusty brick and chipping paint of a dozen off colors, none of which are even manufactured anymore. The signs, some in English and some in Spanish, all offer services few people seek in a modern world. The whole scene looks as dated as a decades-old postcard.

Looking up and down the street in front of La Pachuco, all Victor can think of is a French art house film he saw years ago while on a wrestling tour of Europe. The only thing missing is the sad violin music. Life in Rencor has moved beyond this old neighborhood, and in its wake is nothing but living memories fading more each day.

"Pop," he says to Victor II carefully, "maybe this should be your last Pachuco matinee. At least until business picks back up at the arena, you know?"

"These matinees have been a Victor tradition since before you were born, mijo," his father replies, incredulous.

"I know. I know, but—"

Grandpa Victor abruptly presses his tongue through his mask and raspberries the air, as if to make the point for his grandson.

Victor II frowns heavily at them both.

"You're forgetting what you taught me," he chastises his ancient father, "and what I taught you," he levels at his son. "You wrestle just as hard whether it's five people in the crowd or five thousand."

"Show me five people and I will, Papá!" Victor fires back, frustrated.

Before his father can reply, a little kid, perhaps nine or ten years old, trots up to their table.

He pulls a stack of DVD's out of a backpack that are all messily shrink-wrapped, probably by a home kitchen machine.

The kid shoves the DVD's at Victor.

"See there?" Victor II says to his son. "There's a whole new generation waiting for us! I told you!"

Victor reaches out and dubiously takes the DVD's.

He looks at their equally shoddy covers, probably printed from a regular laser desk printer.

He looks over at the posters beside the theater box office, then back at the DVD's, realizing they're all bootleg copies of the movies playing inside the theater right now.

"Two dollars each, mister!" the kid offers him excitedly. "Three for five if you want!"

Victor stares down at him, speechless.

The kid is trying to sell him pirated copies of their own movies.

Across the table, Victor II's expression drops.

It's visible even through his mask.

"¡Vete al carajo!" Grandpa Victor explodes at the child, leaning forward in his chair and swinging his cane wildly.

"Easy, Tito!" Victor bids his grandfather, reaching up and grabbing the shaft of the cane before it brains the kid.

The budding street merchant turns on his sneaker-clad heels and flees up the street, leaving his short stack of pirate DVD's behind.

As his grandfather unleashes a stream of hoarse curses after the child,

Victor runs his thick, scarred fingertips over the shrink-wrapping sealing the homemade DVD's that bear his elders' likenesses.

He turns and looks at Victor II.

"It's time, Papa," he says.

Victor II bolts from his folding metal chair and for a moment he's thirty years younger, a warrior inside the wrestling ring, poised to strike as he did thousands of times against his enemies.

But he never raises a hand.

Beneath his hood, Victor II's lips part to say something.

They close without a word spoken.

TUESDAY NIGHT'S MAIN EVENT

Victor still drives the two-seater Jaguar convertible painted a glassy burgundy through Rencor with the top down. He keeps the vehicle in good shape, but its age is starting to show. He got it from one of his final sponsors in the last days of his wrestling prime, back when that type of cash and those types of gifts were plentiful.

He barely needs to read street signs; he knows where he is by the sounds and smells alone. In the old districts you hear the clacking of iron-shod horse hooves and the rattling of the carts they draw as often as you hear other car engines. Those sounds all have their own distinct personality, the junk collectors and the fruit and vegetable peddlers and the carriage cabs. He can smell the horses, the manure, the bells jingling.

There are the barkers on the corners and outside the clubs and shops, all laying their best pitch on passersby, some in English, some in Spanish, and the best ones in both. They promise the braver and bolder of the tourist trade exotic delights, bizarre comic relief, the best worst food, and curios of all types.

When he's left those sounds behind Victor knows he's nearing the center of the city. Here the world is underpinned by the constant sounds of construction, jackhammers and backhoes, and the accompanying smell of acrid gravel. Downtown is becoming more and more like an American city every year. The buildings get higher and newer, and any discernible personality or identity is whittled away.

Victor pulls up to the service entrance of the arena. It's the last major piece of old Rencor left downtown. It used to be the largest and most impressive structure for miles, a landmark you could see from anywhere in the city, but now it's obscured in most every direction by tall office and apartment buildings.

In Coliseo Rencor they say you can smell revenge.

Revenge smells an awful lot like bacon-wrapped hot dogs.

Revenge, and bacon-wrapped hot dogs, built the place. There was little more than an old pueblo settlement and a lot of desert when El Barón's grandfather oversaw construction of the Coliseo in the 1950's. Rival promoters ran him out of Mexico after he pushed in on their territories, and his status in the populated corners of America was questionable at best.

He found refuge and then prosperity in a wasteland between both countries neither wanted.

Wrestlers were never hard to find, and if he couldn't find them then he could train whatever dregs he came across as long as they had the size.

But the cagey old man knew such a venue in the middle of nowhere would need a gimmick unto itself, a draw.

That's when he had a simple, brilliant idea.

Coliseo Rencor would be *the* grudge match arena. He'd tour his wrestlers through all the outlying areas where there were a handful of people or more, for months on end, teaching the small crowds their names and faces and establishing bloody feuds between his boys.

But if those same rubes wanted to see the blow-off, the final, epic bout of those feuds, they'd all have to come to the Coliseo.

That simple idea filled the arena, and in the decades that followed built a city around it.

Victor's family was woven into much of that history, and although he's wrestled all over the world the anchor chain pull of Rencor remains inescapable.

It's his home, both geographically and spiritually.

For Victor, entering the empty arena in the middle of the day is like seeing a magnificent work of art with the color drained from its canvas. It looks like an overgrown high school gymnasium, with splinter-filled wooden risers lining each wall. He can see too much of the hideous, permanently stained floor, less parquet and more linoleum glued to bare concrete, which is exposed in several dozen places.

The smells are the same, and comforting. The stale sweat, the musk of heavy canvas that's been soaked through with buckets of sweat and blood. The burnt fat odor of cooked meat that lingers after the sumptuous smell has long gone.

Still, the way some only feel God's presence in a church on Sunday, Victor only feels alive in an arena when it's packed to the rafters on a Saturday night.

Empty folding chairs are arranged around the wrestling ring at the center of the arena. The ring is draped in purple and padded with black. Local businesses and larger companies pay to vomit their logos all over both surfaces.

El Barón stands at ringside, gesturing broadly with a long onyx cigarette holder, shouting instructions in Spanglish to the ring crew who are all bustling about preparing the space for the next show.

Barón is a silver fox with a face that would be handsome save for a large, ruddy nose dominating it. He wears knock-off Hugo Boss suits (albeit expensive knock-offs) which he always covers in a mane-like fur trench coat.

A human skyscraper in drab street clothes hovers over Rencor's dominant wrestling promoter. The near-seven-foot man wears a mask, however he's clearly Caucasian. The mask looks like it might be fashioned from burlap. There's an American flag patch sewn to the forehead, however this flag is a Civil War-era version with thirty-three stars formed into a larger star shape.

Victor zips a red-and-white ring jacket over his shirt and pushes the sleeves up as if he's affixing armor to his body. It's the same jacket he wore hundreds of times while walking to the ring several yards away from where he now stands.

He strides over to the pair.

Victor stares up at the towering gringo. "¿Qué pasa, Wank?" he asks innocently.

"It's *Yank*!" the masked man snarls, as if he's cutting a promo at a live television camera. "*Big* Yank! *The* Big Yank! You know that, little man!"

Victor simply grins. No one knows precisely where El Barón dug up the masked giant, probably some independent wrestling promotion in Texas, but it's clear if he ever was a wrestler he's not anymore. No one has ever seen him step foot in a ring.

And if you're going to don a hood in Victor's town, you better have earned your stripes.

"You're right," Victor assures him. "I do know it."

"Cálmese, Yank," El Barón instructs his muscle. "Victor is only teasing. We're all familia here."

Barón delicately twists a cigarette into the onyx holder. Big Yank hesitates for a moment, but inevitably takes his attention off Victor to light his master's cigarette with a Zippo from his pocket.

"Good to see you, Vic," Barón says before taking a drag.

"You too," Victor says without enthusiasm.

"Are you still pretending you're not taking bookings?" Barón asks him through a cloud of smoke.

Victor waves the smoke away without comment.

Barón smiles, exposing matching lower molars made of pure gold and centered by diamond chips.

"So then you're interested?"

"That depends on your offer."

El Barón laughs. "Smart boy. Smart boy indeed. All right. I need you for Tuesday night."

The promoter might as well have just insulted Victor's mother.

"El Victor doesn't work Tuesdays, hasn't since he was green..." he assures the man in a voice that might as well be his father's or his grandfather's. "If you want me for Friday night's main event, we can talk. Maybe."

Barón waves his cigarette dismissively. "I've got my top técnicos for that. And I have a bunch of gringo talent coming in from the East Coast, to appease all the weekend trade we're getting. What I don't have is a main event for this Tuesday, and I think I can turn it into a good nostalgia night."

"You really don't know anything about this mask, do you?" Victor asks him, and there's almost more pity in his voice than anger.

Although there is a potent amount of anger.

El Barón pinches the bridge of his nose between his fingers as if Victor is giving him a headache.

He sighs.

"Victor...pride took your family a long way in this business, but it's going to start cutting into your bottom line pretty soon here. We can still make a lot of money together; you just have to work with me. You have to accept your place. And where your place is now, not ten years ago. The crowd is changing. You have to change with them."

"No," Victor states flatly.

Big Yank suddenly pokes a cigar-sized finger in his chest. "You don't say 'no' to El Barón," he insists dangerously, the Spanish word sounding like chewed gravel in his mouth.

Victor looks down at the fingertip pressing into his chest.

Then he looks up into Big Yank's cloudy, dull eyes.

"Mierda," El Barón breathes quietly to himself.

In the next instant Victor has Yank's poking finger vice-gripped with his hand and he twists it sharply, unnaturally, and with great power to one side.

The big man growls, his other arm shooting forward at Victor, who quickly grips the exact same finger on Yank's other hand and twists *it* to one side, too.

Big Yank is suddenly on the tips of his booted toes, head tilted back, mewling and suddenly paralyzed by the pain shooting up his arms and through his shoulders and chest.

Victor, still twisting Yank's middle fingers, looks directly at El Barón.

"I don't wrestle for tourists, and I don't work Tuesdays."

"Oh, sure," the promoter says casually, ignoring Yank's plight. "Sure. But let me just say, that ring jacket might still fit you. But it's one of the reasons nothing else does anymore."

Victor doesn't know what to say to that. Fortunately Yank's struggling refocuses his attention.

Victor releases his fingers, but at the same time his right foot smoothly and expertly sweeps the big man's leg out from underneath him.

Big Yank collapses like a demolished building.

Victor looks back at El Barón, poised to leave him with a scathing last line.

Instead he snaps his lips closed and turns on his heels, striding out of the arena.

No one sees him cursing himself.

Victor has never been good at coming up with those action movie-type quips.

Calavera, his arch-nemesis, was always the master of those.

Sometimes it sucks, being an old school good guy.

NUMBER ONE FAN

Gimnasio Victoria was one of the first luchador training academies established in the city of Rencor, founded by the original El Victor in the mid-50's. At its height a hundred students a day filled the large space, training to become luchadores themselves. Those numbers have dwindled like all lucha-related business in town, but the school still does a brisk trade of young hopefuls.

Victor enters the gym, eyes scanning the three rings erected throughout the massive space. Only two of them are classic wrestling rings; they converted the third into a caged octagon to capitalize on the "mixed martial arts" craze of recent years. It helped them pay for the new weightlifting and training equipment occupying its own corner of the gym.

A small class is taking place in one of three training rings. Cousin Hernán is arguing with a big...*big*...tattooed white boy in MMA shorts and five-ounce gloves in the middle of the ring while several students watch from outside.

Victor sticks each pinkie in his mouth and whistles loudly.

Hernán and the cage fighter stop their back-and-forth and turn towards him.

Victor slips through the other students and hops up onto the ring apron.

"What's your problem?" Victor asks the white boy.

"I didn't come here and pay good money...*American* money...to learn this bullshit!"

"Is that a fact?"

Victor slips through the ring ropes and walks across the canvas, silently motioning Hernán to step away.

His cousin does, hiding a grin.

"What did you come here to learn?" Victor asks the cage fighter earnestly.

"How to break into wrestling doing what *I* know how to do!" he challenges back, shadow boxing with a homogenized MMA technique.

Victor scratches the temple of his mask, feigning ignorance.

"I'm confused. Maybe you can show me what you know how to do? Show all of us?"

"You don't want any of me," the cage fighter insists.

"Then me and the local chicas have a lot in common, I think."

That does the trick.

With a snarl, the cage fighter charges at Victor. Dropping his head, he drives a shoulder into Victor's gut and reaches for his legs, trying to take Victor down.

The experienced enmascarado leans forward and thrusts his legs back, out of reach, while looping his arms through and under the younger man's. He forces the cage fighter's arms together behind his back. Victor interlocks his fingers and with a single, powerful heave he suplexes the boy high into the air and brings him crashing down onto his back in the middle of the ring, driving the air out of the cage fighter's lungs.

In the next moment Victor is on top of him, laying across the bigger man's chest, keeping him pinned down.

Victor shoves an elbow into the kid's face and begins grinding it all over as if he's a mongoloid masseuse drunkenly trying to work out a deep kink in a client's back.

As he does, Victor turns his head to speak to the class.

"Now, this is *exactly* the kind of dirty trick a rudo will pull on you in a match. And I don't ever want to see any of you doing stuff like this in here? Okay?"

His local students all nod frantically outside the ring.

Meanwhile, Hernán is laughing himself into a stupor in one of the ring corners.

Victor nods back, satisfied.

He leaps to his feet in one smooth motion.

Below him, the cage fighter frantically rolls out of the ring, clutching his burning face and cursing gutturally. The white boy shakes his head like an irritated hound and looks up at the luchador with rage.

Victor waits, his shoulders squared back and his chest thrust out.

For a moment the cage fighter looks ready to climb back into the ring for round two.

Then, looking at the other students and past Victor at Hernán, he thinks better of it.

"I want my money back!" he shouts at them both, pointing, then turns and stomps away.

"Take a break," Victor instructs the students, turning to his cousin, who's still stifling giggles.

"What's up, carnal?" he greets Victor.

Victor bumps fists with him. "How many paid do we have today?" he asks.

Hernán motions outside the ring. "Not counting the white boy? Thirty. Not amazing, but there's money in the book."

Victor nods, trying not to let the tension show through his mask.

"You're heading out of town again tomorrow, right?" he asks.

Hernán nods. "Yeah...might be for a while too. A new...costumed gig..." he says evasively, eyes turned down.

Victor's cousin still wrestles under the hood of El Lágrima Rojo in Rencor now and then, but that gimmick and the state of the crowds hasn't made him enough money to sustain himself in years. These days he spends much of his time abroad, wrestling in outlandish costumes in Japan. Japanese promoters have always had an affinity for dressing wrestlers in gimmicks taken from American pop culture, everything from horror icons like Freddy Kruger and Leatherface to abstract childish incarnations like My Little Pony.

Hernán has spent most of the year wrestling in a ninja turtle costume. He's a big hit with the kids in Tokyo.

"Be safe then," Victor says.

"Chale."

They clasp hands and embrace before Hernán returns to his class.

"Gypsy!" Victor calls across the gym.

A lithe, toned woman with long dark curls tied into a ponytail pauses after burying a devastating switch kick into one of the gym's hanging heavy bags.

She squints in his direction, then reaches onto a nearby bench and picks up a pair of fire engine red eyeglasses, fitting them onto her pixyish face.

"Vic!" she calls back, smiling.

Gitana Jimenez abandons the heavy bag and trots over to him, expertly uncoiling the wraps around her fist as she does.

"Did you stop by the signing?" she asks him.

"Yeah. Pop decided to make it their finale," he informs her as casually as possible.

Gypsy frowns, but nods understandingly.

"What about El Barón?"

"Nothing worth talking about. Let's head upstairs," Victor says. "Business to attend to."

Gypsy smiles anew. "Right!"

They head for a private elevator concealed behind a workout rack in the back of the musky gym. Gypsy continuously pleads for Victor to replace the lock with a "biometric security system" but he insists on using the old brass key passed down to him from his father and grandfather before him.

Victor resides in the second floor of the gym, a converted hybrid of home, office and shrine of past glories. His father called the same space "headquarters," his grandfather the "lair."

Upon entering the large, open space Gypsy dashes behind a free-standing silk screen in the corner, quickly changing out of her sports top and puffy kickboxing shorts adorned with their Spanish graffiti designs.

She emerges a moment later in street clothes and a long, pressed white lab coat, holding a tablet in one hand and a stylus in the other.

Victor suppresses a grin, always enjoying it when she switches into "assistant mode."

"All right!" she proclaims. "To business!"

"Where are we at with...the auctions?" he asks.

Gypsy refers to her tablet. "I shipped the last batch of items. Most of it to Japan again. And that hotel in Dubai. Payment has cleared for all but one."

Victor, fists pressed into his hips, moves his gaze over the space around them. Walls covered floor to ceiling in three generations of ring event posters and movie lobby cards. Filled to the brim with career mementos and movie props of all shapes and sizes crammed around his regular furniture. Some pieces are covered in plastic awaiting the auction block, other spots a void where all that's left of some departed item is a footprint in the dust.

"What does that put us at with the gym for the month?" he asks her, almost reluctantly.

"Just over seven thousand, boss."

Victor shakes his head. "Still short the operating costs."

"Your other businesses and investments can cover it."

"We have to stop siphoning off good money for this place. It's sinking the rest of my portfolio."

"I know we've talked about it before, but you could put in more octagons, let more MMA fighters train here."

"Yeah, let's have more pendejos like that one I just stretched coming through here."

"Well...you know your masks and ring-worn gear are our best-sellers. And you *further* know which mask would bring in the most money—"

"For the last time, we're not selling the last mask I wore against Calavera." He says, eyeing the torn and battered piece now resting on a ceramic head in a Lucite case.

Gypsy holds up her hands. "It was just a suggestion."

"We're not that desperate," Victor assures her.

He paces through his loft, stopping at a tall glass case housing what's left of the EL ROBOT DEL ESPACIO suit his grandfather fought off in an old serial. The same clunky get-up was repainted decades later to serve as co-host for his father's Saturday night variety show, then half covered in yak fur in the 90s for one of his own made-for-TV epics VICTOR III Y CHARRO-KICKBOXER VS. EL CHUPACABRA ROBOT.

Victor leans his clothed forehead against the glass.

He sighs heavily.

"I'm sorry."

"For what?" Gypsy asks.

"It's just that...I know when you signed on as my assistant you were expecting...you know, excitement and adventure. You thought you were being hired by a hero to do hero's work. And you deserve that. You're way better than cataloguing my old junk for auctions."

With a frustrated exhale, she spots a specific piece of 'old junk' and holds it up for her boss to see. El Victor I and a spectacled, lab-coated professor are being handed medals of appreciation by the mayor of the city in the framed black-and-white publicity photo.

Victor sighs. "Yes, I know...I know the history..."

But Gypsy only stomps over to a framed newspaper on the wall, staring bullets back at him while pointing to the front-page photo of El Victor II and a mustachioed police detective in bell-bottoms escorting a hand-cuffed criminal.

"Jimenezes have been at the sides of Victors since the beginning, I get it." He concedes, arms raised to placate Gypsy. "But you already have more degrees than your grandfather, more fighting skills than your papá. You could be writing your own ticket anywhere. You could be rich."

"This is the life I dreamed of since I was a little girl going to matches and movies. Los Victors were my heroes. If logistics is what I have to do to keep that tradition going than so be it. Money isn't everything." She spits back, partly defiant, partly hurt.

"You sound like my father." Victor replies quietly.

Gypsy smiles broadly. "That's one of the nicest things you've ever said to me."

Victor snorts at that.

"Besides...I think you're the one pining for hero's work, Vic," she says, earnestly.

"Maybe you're right about that..."

Victor turns back to the display case and looks up into the half-mechanical/half-fanged goat-sucker face of the dilapidated movie prop.

"You know...grandpapa used to tell me this thing was real, back when it was just a robot, and that it obeyed his commands because he was the only fighter in the universe to ever defeat it. He'd threaten to send it after me if I didn't go to bed." He chuckles.

"So 20 years later you covered it in fur and fangs to conquer your boyhood fears and defeat it yourself?" Gypsy chides.

"No! That movie...was based on a *reality*."

Gypsy's eyes widen. "You're kidding."

"No...The Calaveras stole this robot suit from storage, paid some quack scientist to hybrid it with some Amazonian vampire aardvark or something. Made it to terrorize goat farmers in the country for...some crazy plan that somehow hinged on terrified goat farmers. I don't know."

"You are so full of shit!"

"*Yeah*," Victor bursts out laughing, unable to sell it a second longer, "we just had no budget on that damn movie so we recycled anything we could." He snorts as Gypsy punches him in the arm.

"Thing is...sometimes, as more years go by, I think my family can't remember what was a publicity stunt and what was real."

"Do you actually believe in monsters, though? You've never told me."

"I've never seen one. All I have is stories and some old pictures that always look fake."

"But do *you* believe?"

"I believe if there were monsters, there aren't anymore, at least not werewolves and gorilla mermaids and robot chupacabras and...whatever. They all went away."

"Maybe people got too bad for them. We became the monsters."

"Or maybe Tito and Papá defeated them all...Or maybe it was all a *work*."

"*Work* as in wrestling speak for 'a lie' right?"

"You're picking it up fast."

"That's what those fancy degrees are for. But yeah. A *work*. Knowing the studio people and wrestling promoters, equally possible."

"Still," Victor says, glancing back at the makeshift warehouse full of genuine trophies and fake props, indistinguishable from one another. "I'd fight an army of robot chupacabras right now if it meant not having to read one more past due notice."

"Be careful what you wish for, boss," Gypsy warns him.

Again, Victor snorts.

"If wishes were horses we'd all be eating carne asada, Gypsy."

MUM'S THE WORD

It's already been a shitty day for Gus, and now he's standing at the perimeter created by the hazardous waste team, staring at a crater-sized hole in one of the city's most prominent buildings.

La Museo de Rencor was built back in the day when real money flowed through the city and a couple of rich marks wanted to import some genuine culture.

After losing some treasures in high-profile robberies (largely due to the Calaveras clan), the museum had problems getting collections on loan, and has since devolved into more of a tourist trap — local wrestling and movie studio memorabilia co-mingling with genuine antiques and artifacts, and an underpaid, undertrained staff that has long since forgotten what's real and what's fake.

You wouldn't think such a "museum" would be worth breaching with a big-rig gas tanker in the middle of the night for an overly catastrophic smash-and-grab, but evidently someone did...

In addition to theft and destruction of public property, apparently the tank itself was pierced in the collision and vented whatever gas it contained, causing a public health hazard as well.

All Gus wants in that moment is flan.

Lots of flan.

His favorite spot for flan isn't far from the museum, in fact, and it's 24-hours.

Instead he waits patiently until one of his men in a hermetically sealed suit and gas mask approaches him from inside the building.

"It's clean, Captain," the man announces. "All readings we took are nominal. Nothing noxious or dangerous detected."

"Oh, good," Gus says dryly. "We can investigate now."

It's dark inside the Egyptian wing of the museum. Gus and his team have to spot everything with flashlights.

"The truck took out the wiring," another one of his investigators informs him. "Killed the lights and the cameras in this wing. We don't know if that was intentional or not."

"Pretty damn convenient," Gus comments. "Was anyone hurt?"

"One of the guards was doing his rounds. He has a concussion and a dislocated collarbone from fallen debris, but he'll make it."

"Is that the end of the good news?" Gus asks.

"A lot of this stuff was on loan from way back and a lot of it is gone, Captain."

"Priceless and irreplaceable?"

"Yep. They knew just where to hit."

"Have someone run down to El Farolito and get me two large flans, will you?"

"Uh...sure, Captain. I thought you were dieting, though—"

"Piss on you and my diet! Tell them it's for Gus the Bus. I don't care."

"Yes, sir. Sorry."

"And while I'm waiting it would be just perfecto if someone had a rundown of what's missing? Anyone?"

Another one of his men, a nervous thirty-something in a cheap suit and carrying a clipboard sprints forward.

"Uh...two showcases in the wing were ransacked, Captain. They contained artifacts, an array of necklaces, medallions, and amulets of... 'ancient and mysterious purpose and origin'...at least that's what the plaque in front of the smashed cases says. We'll have to get photos of the actual pieces from the museum."

"What else?"

"Well..." the officer begins uncertainly. "It's weird..."

"What's weird?"

"I'm not sure how to—"

"¡Dios mío!" Gus tilts his head back and shouts. "I'll look for myself. Go check on my flans."

Without waiting for a response, Gus grabs a flashlight out of the hand of the nearest investigator holding one and strikes off into the wrecked museum wing.

"And someone get this damn truck out of here!" he yells back at his team as he awkwardly slides his large frame around a wheel well the size of a church door.

The interior isn't as bad as he thought it would be, but it isn't far off. Every step chews gravel and glass shards. Gus traipses carefully past the pilfered showcases, both thoroughly cleaned out just like his officer said. He shines his light on a large freestanding object in the back.

It's a sarcophagus, an ancient coffin taller than him and obviously hand-carved from stone, the sides decorated with Egyptian hieroglyphs.

The lid of the sarcophagus is missing.

A strip of decayed cloth hanging from a rough hewn edge of the frame sways in the breeze from outside.

Otherwise the coffin is empty.

Gus shines his light at the floor in front of the ancient burial vessel.

Not just an empty sarcophagus, but—

His breath catches in his throat.

This is exactly the kind of thing a police captain would've once called in a—

An idea begins bubbling in the back of Gus's brain. He realizes he's been thinking about a scenario like since his meeting with Medianoche weeks ago. A daring museum heist in the Egypt wing is the perfect excuse.

"No one else go in!" he shouts back at his men. "I need to make a call."

· · · ·

Thirty minutes later Gus is staring at the soiled bottoms of two empty aluminum flan containers, feeling bad about himself now that the rush of eating them is over, and Victor's Jaguar pulls up to the scene.

Victor dashes from behind the wheel wearing his hood, a vintage Victor II t-shirt, silk pajama pants and flip-flops.

"Sorry to rouse you from bed in the middle of the night," Gus says, looking over his outfit.

"You said it was an emergency!" Victor shoots back, almost frantic.

"I don't recall that."

"You absolutely did."

"Then I misspoke," Gus says evenly. "What we have is an apparent burglary in the museum here."

Victor stares past him at the large hole in the building.

"Burglaries aren't what they used to be."

Gus grunts. "Nothing is. Still and all, my department hasn't handled a burglary like this in...I can't even remember. We've gotten too used to mopping up bodies and shootings."

"So what?"

"So, that's why I called you."

"I don't do this kind of work anymore. You know that."

"*Nobody* does this kind of work anymore. I gave Medianoche his papers a couple of weeks ago, in fact."

Victor is speechless for several moments.

"You fired the old man? You couldn't let him retire with a gold watch or something?"

"You know he never would've left on his own two feet. He was a real hero."

"And I'm not?" Victor asks, his voice rising suddenly.

Gus holds up a hand. "I didn't mean that. All right?"

The captain warily remembers the sting when Victor left the ranks of the Rencor PD Auxiliary Patrol and convinced his father to do the same. The masked man saw the writing on the wall, and thought he could take the lucha-hero and the Victor family into the 21st century in other ways. He was as wrong as the rest of the masked crime-fighters who stayed behind, but at least he left the force with his dignity and persona intact.

"I understand why you left. You were right. There was nothing left for you, for any of you."

"Then why call me now?"

"Because you spent years fighting one of the greatest art thieves from the greatest art thief family of our time. Which, since you also got that art thief exiled, means you're the closest thing I've got to him. I want your opinion."

"Like I told a guy earlier," Victor says. "I don't work Tuesday nights."

"It's the Egypt wing," Gus tells him.

Victor's eyes can't help lighting up a little.

"Two showcases of ancient medallions and necklaces were ransacked, and...something else."

"...what else?"

"Just have a look."

"What else, Gus?" Victor demands.

"How many Egypt-type movies did your pop do?" the Captain presses. "Huh?"

Gus holds up his flashlight, offering it to the enmascarado.

"Just your opinion," Gus insists. "That's all. Ten minutes."

Victor hesitates, then snatches it from him and Gus leads him past the smashed cases of stolen amulets to the large, empty sarcophagus. A few moments later the flashlight beam falls upon the first footprint in the debris dust.

He's excited at first, then confused.

The print is impossibly small, almost like a child's, and contorted.

He spots another that looks like the other foot was dragging the second foot behind it.

A disabled child driving a big rig through a wall to steal from a museum?

Not likely.

Victor follows the footprints in the dust, Gus directly behind him, backtracking rather than letting them lead him out of the museum. They end several yards deep into the dark recess of the Egyptian wing.

They also end at the foot of the propped-up sarcophagus.

Victor shines his light from its interior to the footprints at its base.

He realizes they don't end at the lip of the sarcophagus.

They begin there.

It's as if someone or *something* walked out it.

"Well? What do you think?"

"It's a mummy," Victor says, in awe. "It's a mummy."

"Oh, you gotta be fucking kidding me now," Gus curses under his breath.

"A real one. It...either they, the burglars, they freed it or it got free after they smashed through the wall. Either way, it walked out of here. On its own. It walked."

"A mummy?" Gus asks again. "Three flans...I should've asked for three flans."

Victor nods. "*La momia*...Just like...they used to talk about. My pop. My grandpa. A mummy. Like the old days."

"I knew it. I just didn't want to...or couldn't believe it."

Despite the disturbing, almost ludicrous news, Gus can't help grinning a bit to himself.

It's those last four words spoken by Victor.

"Like the old days."

PART TWO

RUDO

TEN YEARS AGO...THE OTHER LOCKEROOM

El Mil Calaveras III is nursing over a dozen serious injuries after his epic, history-making El Perdedor Abandona La Ciudad (or "Loser Leaves Town") match with El Victor III. His knuckles are busted from throwing punches. His skull is concussed. But the only body part he's acutely aware of as he sits backstage in his private locker room is his shoulder; it didn't suffer any damage in the match, but it feels gnawingly, achingly empty. It's where the championship belt should be resting at that moment, but isn't.

Calavera can hear his grandfather somewhere outside the locker room, screaming in his gravelly voice at the reporters and errant fans who are cheering the family's defeat and Calavera's banishment from the city and its wrestling rings.

His father is standing over him, Calavera's blood on his double-breasted suit, and probably some of Victor's father's blood as well (the two older men brawled several times at ringside during the match). He wore that same suit to the first match in which his son donned the family's signature skull mask and became El Mil Calaveras III.

Calavera tells himself he can't look up because he cracked a vertebra in his neck, but the truth is he can't meet his father's eyes in that moment.

Instead he fills his head with plots, schemes and torments he's going to unleash on Victor and his family, in and out of the ring. His vengeance for this defeat, this disgrace, is going to make headlines.

It's going to—

"It's over," his father says through the same mask Calavera him-self wears.

Now Cal looks up at the older man, who is at that moment looming as large and imposing as he did when Calavera was a boy.

"¿Qué?"

"It's over," his father repeats. "I can see your eyes spinning with revenge. There won't be any. Not now. You agreed to this. You have to leave."

"I've agreed to a lot of things. So have you—"

"This isn't some judge's sentence in a court!" his father fires back, making both instruments of law sound like the most contemptible, forget-table of things. "This is La Coliseo. This is unbreakable. And this is why in my day we never did matches like this. There's no coming back. I'd rather...I'd rather you'd lost the mask."

Those words cut deeper and pain Calavera in a way no ring injury ever could. Yet even in that moment, still dripping with blood and filled with adrenaline, he knows his father is right. There are only a few laws the Calaveras respect, and this is one of them.

He has to leave Rencor.

Forever.

SAY HELLO TO THE BAD GUY

All real FBI agents look like extras in a movie about FBI agents. In the same way, the FBI in real-life is a lot like a movie about the FBI without any of the scenes involving the stars or the villains.

That is to say, for the most part it's boring background shit.

A group of such agents sits around a conference table in an FBI field office located in the heart of Chicago.

Their names aren't important, and neither are they.

"Five minutes late."

"Seriously, who are we waiting for again?"

"Some kind of consultant. Civilian. A profiler."

"I thought that only happened on TV?"

"ASAC's bring them in when they get desperate. Like, *really* desperate."

"Think of it like our case is having a midlife crisis and went out and bought a Porsche."

"Right. Fancy, but useless."

"Pretty much."

"So who is he? The profiler?"

"Some kind of reformed art thief, I guess. I heard he's the guy who tracked down those stolen Renoirs. You remember, like five of 'em, all serial burglaries from high-end private collectors? His identity is supposedly classified. His codename is...*Tío Chango*? I think?"

"He has a codename?"

"Wait, why don't *we* get codenames?"

"I totally want a codename."

"Doesn't 'Tío Chango' mean 'Uncle Monkey?'"

"My dad used to drink this gross chocolate milk called Tio—"

"Gentlemen!"

All heads turn towards the door, where a blonde WASP in a pressed pantsuit with FBI credentials clipped to her lapel is suddenly watching them.

"I'm Special Agent Stella O'Shaughnessy. Just in from Connecticut."

"Are you who we're waiting for?"

"You're five minutes late, you know."

"Are you Tío Chango?"

"Doesn't Tío Chango mean 'Uncle Monkey?'"

"I'm liaison to the asset in question," Special Agent O'Shaughnessy informs them.

With that, she gestures grandly but without enthusiasm towards the door.

This is when the bland real-life FBI becomes a movie about the FBI.

"The Asset" might as well be entering the room in slow motion with an ominous soundtrack. Towering, barrel-chested, he cuts a figure that silences everyone in the room instantly, even before they see the mask.

His face and head are hooded by a máscara designed to resemble a Dia de los Muertos skull. It's purple with black and blue flames, the number "1000" emblazoned across the forehead. He wears a deep royal-purple double-breasted suit to compliment the hood, along with a purple-and-gold flame tie and matching pocket square. The heels of his sharkskin gaucho boots are also menacing gold skulls.

"This is your asset, gentlemen," Special Agent O'Shaughnessy says. "Codename Tío Chango. AKA El Mil Calaveras...the Third to be exact. For the sake of expediency you can call him 'Cal'—"

"No...they can't," Calavera corrects her smoothly.

He walks past the seated agents, removing a long stogy and a skull-shaped cigar cutter from inside his coat. He pulls its steel jaws apart and the skull bites the end off of the cigar. Replacing it in his pocket, Cal's fingers produce a long match.

"There's no smoking in here—" one of the agents begins, but the words somehow die on his lips.

Cal strikes the match and lights his cigar, waving the match out and tossing it away as he widens his stance at the head of the conference table.

Calavera deftly flips open a file on the tabletop in front of him.

"Nine priceless works of art," he recaps for the agents in a booming, low-temblor voice as smooth as it is forceful and confident. "Seven of them stolen from the most high-profile museums across Europe and Asia, one from The Met in New York..." He nods to Stella, and she smirks and bows her head slightly at the acknowledgment of her introduction and first contribution to the case. "...and the ninth taken from the Art Institute here in Chicago. Which is where you come in. Interpol reached out. They've been made to look like the incompetents they are for the past year, and they've got nothing. Neither did you. Until now."

Cal takes a long drag from his cigar.

They all notice he's wearing three identical rings side-by-side on the last three fingers of his right hand.

Each one is fashioned like a miniature championship wrestling belt.

"The mastermind behind these thefts has been taunting Interpol specifically, daring them to catch him."

"—or her," Stella corrects him.

Cal pauses, at first annoyed by the interruption and then, as he stares back at her, overtaken by a slow grin.

"It's personal," he continues. "That would suggest someone Interpol locked up—"

"We've combed through Interpol's files for known international burglars—"

The agent stops speaking and starts coughing as Cal blows a cloud of cigar smoke in his face.

And he looks cool doing it.

"However," Cal continues, "the thief possesses an intimate knowl-edge of Interpol procedure. He *or she* slipped through their last two stakeouts totally undetected. In addition to that, if he *or she* were some-one they'd put away their motivation wouldn't just be just to make them look stupid, it'd be revenge. And real revenge...hurts. Deeply. No, this is someone who wants to prove they're right and Interpol is wrong. This was a former agent, one who was fired, and did not take it well at all."

"Well, we can...check on who was dismissed within the last two years from Interpol Europe and made a lot of noise about it—"

"I already did," Cal informs them. "His name is Pierre Moncan. He's down the hall right now."

Cal reaches inside his jacket and presents them with a flash drive.

"Here's his confession," Cal says, placing the flash drive down and sliding it across the tabletop. "Special Agent O'Shaughnessy and I arrived on time. That's what I was doing for the past five minutes."

"How'd you get him to confess in five minutes?"

"I offered him a cigar."

Cal punctuates the statement by twisting out the lit end of his own cigar in the center of the FBI file on the table, singing every page.

He leaves it there, rising from the smoking ashes like a miniature grave marker.

"Jesus."

"Wait...I...we...aren't you just a profiler?"

Cal shrugs, having already stepped away from the head of the conference table.

"I wanted to find out if he was better than me," he says, walking past them towards Stella and the door.

He winks at her.

Stella's eyes somehow manage to give him the middle finger.

"He wasn't," Cal announces to them as he exits the room.

Stella watches him go, the only one unimpressed with his theatrics and his accomplishments.

She turns back to the other agents.

He isn't two seconds out the door before the agents around the table are Googling his name on their smartphones.

Soon one of them is showing the others a video of a younger Cal wreaking havoc in a wrestling arena.

The others crowd around him, awestruck.

Stella rolls her eyes.

"Well then. Glad we could be of help," she says, throwing them a mock salute before she exits the room as well.

Cal is already lighting another cigar when Stella catches up with him in the hall.

She reaches over and snatches away the match before he can strike it.

"There really is no smoking in this building," she assures him.

Cal is silent for a moment.

Then: "Anything for you, Stella."

He slips the cigar back inside his jacket.

"Can I buy you breakfast?" Cal asks her.

"I'm not in the mood to deal with a shitty Chicago diner trying to pass off pancake syrup as true maple," she says, and for just a moment the New England accent she's long since overcome slips through.

"I notice you didn't mention the tip *I* got on Moncan," she says. "Or that I tracked him to that rat-hole hotel he was hiding out in and collared him?"

"The profile was right. And I did get his confession."

"How, by the way?"

"You didn't watch?" Cal asks her.

"I was keeping everybody else away from the room."

"Ask me again sometime."

Stella's about to say more, but her cell phone rings and she stops walking to answer it.

Cal waits impatiently, unbuttoning his jacket and sliding his hands inside the pockets of his slacks.

He's barely listening, and really only tunes back in when Stella says, "Right. We'll be there."

She ends the call.

"Where to now?" he asks.

"Have you ever heard of a border town called Rencor?"

It's rare moments like these when Cal wishes his family's mask covered more of his mouth and eyes.

Just the same, he tries to keep a face made of stone.

"I think you know well that I have, Stella. Or am I to believe you haven't poured through every scrap of info on me like a diligent agent?"

Stella smirks again. "I just wanted to see your face. Which, of course, I never do."

"What about Rencor?" Cal demands.

"The two of us, a plane ride, and some stolen Egyptian artifacts."

"I'm going to need that match back now," is all he says to her in reply.

nOn-PRODIGAL SON

Rencor's airport is really no more than a small *airfield* twenty minutes outside the city. Several of its runways are still tightly packed dirt, but are actually smoother than the long-neglected paved ones. The entire field is crewed by a single tower, a single ninety-year-old customs agent who literally rides his donkey to work, and a rickety shack in which passengers can buy horchata, agua fresca, and handmade empanadas from the same old woman who's been making them there since the strip only serviced a single Cessna belonging to El Barón the First.

Since the revitalization of the inner city, a shiny new international airport has been under constant construction on the other side of town. In the meantime, the airfield mostly services private planes, and the odd commercial commuter jet from both sides of the border. At its height they'd see party planes full of Asian and Arab businessmen flying in for the matches every weekend, but even with El Barón's father taxing and up-charging that money to death he never upgraded the airstrip itself.

"My family used to have our own jet here," Calavera explains to Stella as the two begin to disembark their small airbus.

"Let me guess...shaped like a skull?"

Cal laughs, pausing at the open-air platform that meets the door. "Of course not. How would that even be aerodynamically possible? It was just a Lear jet painted with, like, three hundred skulls. The paint job alone was worth fifty grand."

Stella sighs. "My life was so much better before I knew people like you existed."

"You mean 'after,' of course," Cal assures her confidently.

His first step down the stairs to the tarmac isn't as confident.

"So what happened? To your family's jet?" Stella chides, growing impatient at their snail's pace.

Cal takes a deep breath. "Transitional cash flow issues after I...left the city."

"You were still wrestling, though."

"It wasn't the same." Cal replies, stopping again mid stairwell. "All the American promoters wanted me to unmask, so that was a dead-end market. Japanese promoters...well, Japan is practically an alternate reality. Not to mention the Yakuza are bigger crooks than I ever was, if you can believe that. And everywhere in-between the money was smaller than I was used to."

As they approach the final steps, Cal stops suddenly.

"What's wrong?" Stella asks, her hand reflexively inching closer to her holstered pistol.

"Not a thing," he says softly.

She realizes he's just breathing in and out, deeply.

"No place smells like this," he explains, sounding almost dreamlike, using the sudden intake of scent to delay the moment he'll have to step back into a world he thought he'd left forever. "It's like the desert and the city at the same time. And the cooking smells...ay Dios mío...no city in the world cooks like Rencor, or as much."

"It smells like empanadas and I think it's coming from that shack over there," Stella corrects him.

"It's more than that!" he snaps at her. "That's the ghost of a million-and-one bacon-wrapped hot dogs made at the arena, my dear. The whole city used to smell like that on Saturday night."

"That sounds delightful, Cal. Desiccated hog flesh is my scent, after all. Can we go now? Please?"

He looks down at her, a sadness in his partially textile shielded eyes.

She suddenly feels like, for the first time since they began working together, he's somehow disappointed in her.

Stella is surprised by how dark that notion makes her feel.

"I'm sorry, all right?" she relents. "I get this is a big deal for you, coming back. I obviously don't have the reference to appreciate how big a deal, but you gotta give me that it's a pretty weird, specific kind of reference, your life."

Calavera considers that, half-shrugs.

"Fair."

With another deep, bracing breath, Calavera finally sets foot back on Rencor soil.

There's a Rencor PD squad car waiting for them at the edge of the runway.

Cal stops again, this time his whole body stiffening.

"What now?" she asks.

"They couldn't have sent an unmarked car?"

"Look where we are, Cal. What's the problem?"

"Old instincts, I guess. I suddenly feel like this was all an elaborate trap and they're about to spring it on me."

"If anyone tries to spring anything on *us* then it's my government-sanctioned duty to shoot them. All right?"

"That's slightly reassuring, I admit."

"Think of this way. You've gone from being chased by these cars to being chauffeured by them."

Cal actually grins at that, just a little.

"I do enjoy the perks of this gig."

DUST-UPS OLD AND NEW

Rencor Police Headquarters is less like a modern law enforcement building and more like an old west sheriff's office multiplied several dozen times in size. Most government buildings have small barriers lining the entrances to prevent wayward vehicles from crashing through; Rencor's Police HQ is ribbed with pylons the size of redwoods, having been fortified against things like giant robot and hovercraft attacks.

In Gus's office, Victor idly edges the bottom drawer of the captain's desk open while he's not looking.

"Qué coño," he marvels, then whistles at the sight of the candy wrapper graveyard in the drawer.

Gus turns from the files he was examining and kicks the drawer shut. "Mind your manners!"

Victor laughs. "I think you look good, Gustavo. You worry too much"

"Yeah, well, none of us are in our prime anymore."

"I'm close enough for my own comfort," Victor assures him.

"Let's get down to business. I've got three reports from the old districts of 'shambling-guy-covered-in-bandages' sightings!"

"From anyone who isn't a borrachón?"

"One stone cold sober tourist."

"That's not exactly a smoking gun."

"But you're here. You're asking. You're obviously interested. Did you tell your pop?"

Victor shakes his head slowly.

Gus frowns. "Why not?

"Because I don't want to get his hopes up. No one misses hero work more than him. I ruined it for him once. I don't want to do it again."

"Victor, you did what you could to keep it going. Leaving the force was the right choice. Maybe you made a bad call afterwards, maybe you didn't. But you tried."

It's obvious Vic doesn't want to talk about that particular episode of his past. "So is this everything you called me over here for?"

"...No," Gus says carefully. "There's something...*else*. Some of the missing artifacts must have shown up on a bigger radar screen than ours. The FBI is sending us a consultant, or profiler or something. An expert on museum thefts."

"Why?"

"He's...uniquely qualified. You know the mat and the monsters, this guy knows these kinds of heists. It'll be...a good fit, I think."

"Why is your voice as tight as a guitar string?"

"What? Nothing. No reason. I just want you to keep an open mind, that's all. Drastic times call for drastic measures and all of that. I think if you—"

Gus is still talking, but he abruptly becomes aware Victor is no longer listening.

He's staring out the windows of Gus's office, suddenly transfixed, and that fixation slowly transforms from shock to confusion to abject horror.

"What?" Gus follows his rapidly hardening gaze out the window.

Calavera and an attractive yet slightly severe looking blonde woman wearing FBI credentials are milling at the opposite end of the squad room.

"Oh...Victor, wait—" Gus begins, but it's miles past too late.

"Calavera!" Victor yells, and it sounds like a primal war cry.

Victor bolts through the door of Gus's office and tears across the squad room, vaulting over two desks in a single bound and leaping up onto the old, cracked wooden railing partitioning the area.

Calavera looks up and his eyes lock on that red mask plastered with its face-sized "V" and in the next moment his own limited expression is an exact mirror of Victor's.

He abandons his casual stance and launches himself forward, suddenly running full-tilt at the man who exiled him from Ciudad Rencor.

Victor leaps from the railing in a picture-perfect *plancha* dive, as if he were descending from the top-rope of a wrestling ring.

"Cal! Hey! What the hell?" Stella yells after him, her hand going to the grip of her holstered pistol, but not drawing the weapon.

El Victor and El Mil Calaveras collide like not a day, an hour, a single moment has passed since they were young lions battling for supremacy in the ring. They tie up and are spun into a tornado-like circle as they grapple for position and advantage.

Though it's ferocious, one thing becomes almost immediately clear — they are no longer two young lions meeting for the first time. They've wrestled hundreds of matches, and even in their shocked, angry, instinctive states know each other as well or better than any two opponents ever have.

Victor throws a familiar series of forearm shots that Calavera either ducks or blocks with his own forearms. When Cal responds by launching a booted foot at Victor's groin, a move that worked at least half the time in their feuding days, Victor deflects it with a raised knee as if his conscious mind, the bit of it left unhindered by bloodlust, is expecting it. Calavera tries to scoop Victor's body up to slam him to the floor, but the técnico blocks it by wrapping his leg around Calavera's. Victor immediately tries to reverse the hold and execute the same slam only to have Calavera block it in the exact same way.

It's like watching a pair of fraternal twins try to kick each other's ass.

They finally give each other vicious two-handed shoves backwards, and stumble to keep their footing. Victor's frustration overwhelms him. He curls his fist into a tight ball and launches a punch into Calavera's face that connects flush, dazing the rudo and breaking the stalemate.

Neither of them realize they're now surrounded by cops, but rather than interceding and arresting them both the entire uniformed crowd is watching and cheering as if they're all in the Coliseo.

"What the hell are you all doing?" Gus's voice finally booms at his men. "Break them up! ¡Rápido! Now!"

Two-dozen police officers are torn from their trance. Half seize Victor and pull him into the squad room while the other half drag Calavera back towards the entrance.

Gus seizes Victor by the arms while across a sea of bodies Stella roughly forces her smaller frame between all of the uniforms to get to Cal — her charge and responsibility.

"I always could make you throw a closed fist like a rudo, Victor!" Calavera taunts him expertly. "But you *still* hit like a bitch!"

Soon neither man can see his old foe through the crowd.

"Will you shut up and come on!" Stella orders him. "We don't need this. *I* don't need this!"

She leads Calavera out of the precinct by the arm, Cal mostly backpedaling as his attention remains on the squad room.

The mass of uniformed bodies keeps the roadblock between the two intact long enough to give Calavera and Stella time to make their exit.

Meanwhile, Victor is pacing back and forth in front of Gus in the squad room like a caged animal.

"Victor, let me explain!" Gus pleads with him.

"Explain what?" Victor demands, manic with rage and confusion. "I don't know how you *caught* him or when, but you better reinstate my old badge and swear me in because *I'm* the one who's going to interrogate him! He's violated the stipulation of our last match! He's destroyed the museum! He's stolen priceless artifacts! He's released a mummy! He's...he's..."

"NO! You don't understand, he's here—"

"He's not supposed to be here! Not ever! I beat him! I beat him once and for all!"

With the commotion in the rearview, the officers barring the entrance to the squad room begin to break up and return to their tasks.

"Victor, you have to calm down and let me tell you—"

But Victor is already leaping over the railing again and charging towards the door.

"Where is he?" he yells, grabbing a rookie cop attending the door.

"He took off in a car with that blonde—"

"I'll find him!" he yells back with utter certainty. "If he stays in my city, I'll find him!"

"Victor, will you *please* let me explain!" Gus pleads, the last few words shouted at the door closing slowly behind Victor's disappearing form.

Gus sighs. "No, this is still a good idea," he insists to himself quietly.

"It's a good idea."

"It's a good idea."

"It's a *good* idea..."

THE RETURN OF EL JEFE

You have to earn the right to drink in the Pandemonio bar. It's not an easy status to acquire. Lacing up a hood and bashing a good guy wrestler over the head with a folding steel chair isn't enough. Hatching some wild scheme to hold the city hostage for ransom that gets foiled by a masked hero inside of a week and ends up in the lower corner of the back of the Sunday paper doesn't even merit consideration.

No, the bar in the Pandemonio is reserved for front-page villains.

It's where the absolutely best of the bad, the legends, toast their dastardly deeds and drink their hard-earned villainous glory.

The original El Mil Calaveras earned his stool in the late 1950's after defeating The Cyclone, at the time the biggest masked gringo wrestling star in America. Grandpa Cal peeled Cyclone's drab, ugly goat-skin-looking mask off the man's bloody head and brought it back to hang behind the bar, where it remains to this day, the first of many defeated heroes to become trophies in that particular place of dishonor. Next to the mask is a framed copy of a newspaper with the headline, "EL MIL CALAVERAS NABS WIFE OF FAMED AMERICAN WRESTLER, FLEES TEXAS." That's how the villain drew him to Rencor for the showdown.

And although the original El Victor had rescued the woman and made his own headlines returning her to the bandaged gringo worker, Calavera managed to hide the stolen mask, keeping it for himself.

His son, Calavera II, pulled up a stool next to his legendary father in the early 1970's, after kidnapping the most famous, and most beautiful telenovela soap opera star of the time and trussing her up on a weather vane at the top of the tallest building in Rencor during a thunder storm. It was all, of course, a diversion while his minions executed his plan to steal a priceless collection of Japanese ceramics from the museum.

Victor II had to commandeer a helicopter to rescue the girl ("Which the idiota crashed because he didn't know how to fly in the first place!" Calavera II was always fond of reminding his son when telling the story).

It was an event that made the city and its wrestling worldwide news, even if the Victor family took all the credit in the end.

Calavera III, the newest generation villain in the family, was the youngest of any of them to be granted a place at the bar, not because of his family's legacy, but because his feud with the Victor of his age returned the family and the city to glory after several waning years. Post-national cable television and at the dawn of the internet age, he became a more widely known rudo than any of them, even if his father's and grandfather's golden age of prestige and mystique had passed.

The third-generation star of the villainous clan took it corporate, branding their trademark skulls a thousand different ways and elevating the family law firm, their longstanding "cover" business, to heights unseen as well.

Pandemonio is located on the shadiest corner of the section of Rencor known as Poquito Xibalba. A lot of locals say "Li'l Zee" is the point in Rencor at which Mexico unofficially ends and America unofficially begins. Despite decades of urbanization, you can still see the scars of the original pueblo settlement in Li'l Zee. Pieces of gutted, graffitied adobe wall stand like tombstones between many of the modern buildings.

Several original structures have been converted into rustic bars and eating-houses, historical preservations by default.

It's no surprise Li'l Zee evolved into the rudo side of town, where no técnico, cop, or wayward tourist is welcome.

Villains are always the last to accept change.

On Pandemonio's stage, a battered crescent raised three feet off the ground and bordered by high chicken wire woven through with the barbed variety, Mariachis from Hell launch into their third blistering set of the night. The leather-vest-and-leather-sombrero-clad, electrified perverters of classical mariachi music have been the house band for the last three years, since the bar's former headliners, Los Torpedoes, took down a bank on the wrong side of the border and never came back.

The bar is thinly populated tonight, as it is most nights these days; legendary villains being in short supply. But their stools are never occupied. They stand empty, as monuments, both waiting and permanently retired.

The tables filling the rest of the space are more densely packed, loaded down with rudos on the come-up and on their way out, along with every other assortment of non-mask-wearing wrestling lowlife from crooked referees to rough-and-tumble ring crews. They play poker for every form of currency and five-finger fillet with wicked-looking blades that have tasted the blood of combat.

The newest breed to fill the space is the never-was. These are the rudos who weren't really criminals or masterminds, just dedicated wrestlers with a necessary flair for the dastardly, but who turned to crime after being screwed and shunned time and time again by promoters like El Barón. They're Rencor's newest, most embittered, and possibly last generation of villains.

It's after midnight when Calavera enters Pandemonio for the first time since the night before his Loser-Leaves-Town match against Victor.

When Calavera makes the scene, it all freezes.

Every game and conversation stops immediately.

All heads turn towards the door.

Even the music ceases.

He's chosen the flaming green version of his signature skull hood, and a double-breasted suit to match. The skull heels of Cal's gaucho boots are crusted with diamonds and sparkle brilliantly even in the dim lights of the bar. The skull pinned to his matching green flame tie is also one large, brilliant diamond.

Cal stops just past the threshold, both playing the part of returning royalty in Hell and savoring their baffled, reverent, and above all frightened reactions to his sudden presence after so many years.

After the appropriate pause, Cal delicately tugs the lapels of his suit and turns towards the bar, heels clacking like tiny gunshots.

"Calaveras Brand," he informs the bartender in a deep, neutral voice that nevertheless brooks no argument.

The kid looks barely in his twenties, covered in tattoos and piercing.

He doesn't share the expression of most in the bar.

He just shrugs. "Never heard of it. We only serve cerveza and tequila here, man."

"¡Tranquilo, idiota!" a grizzled voice shouts from the back, outraged.

An old man hobbles out to the kid and smacks him in the head with a withered yet steady hand.

"Shit!" the kid curses. "What? What did I do?"

In answer the old man smacks him again, grabs him by the inked bicep and ushers him away from the bar, taking his place with great effort.

"Lo siento, Señor Calavera," the old bartender begs Cal, practically bowing. "My grandson. He's new. And ignorant."

Cal waves away the offense magnanimously.

The old man is already delving deep beneath the bar, rummaging hastily, anxiously, his eyes trying to never leave Calavera's out of fear of disrespecting the seemingly resurrected villain.

He comes up with a skull-shaped box, which he holds with great reverence. Placing it on the bar top, the veteran server pulls apart the two sides of the skull's face to reveal a bottle within.

As the bartender fills a tumbler with a finger of rich golden liquid, Cal glances back at the middle of the barroom. The evening's festivities are slowly starting back up again, but many eyes remain on him.

Behind the bar, the old man limps over to a large terrarium erected among the shelves of bottles. The glass encasement is irradiated with blue, flickering light and filled with live scorpions.

Without hesitation, the bartender reaches through the top of the terrarium and pinches one of the vicious creatures by its pointed tail, removing it.

He carefully ferries the scorpion over to the bar top where he drops it into Cal's glass, immersing it in the liquor.

"It's an honor to serve you again, Señor Calavera," the old man says, half-bowing again as he backs away.

Cal reaches out and takes up the glass, feeling all of those eyes boring into it and him anew.

He knocks it back and drains the liquor quickly, moving the rim away from his lips before the drunken scorpion touches them.

Cal rolls the liquid around his tongue and slowly swallows.

Then, in one quick motion, he knocks the glass back again and fires the soaked scorpion into his mouth, quickly crunching it up with his teeth.

He swallows what's left, too.

Cal turns the glass upside-down and replaces it on the bar top amidst low, awe-struck murmurs from the crowd.

"It's good to be back, my friend," he says to the bartender.

"¡Jefe!" a tiny, helium-laced voice cries to him from the crowd. "It can't be you, can it?"

Cal squints through the din.

A minuscule figure parts from the crowd of tables in the center of the bar. He's a little person, no more than three feet tall. His limbs and fingers are perfectly proportionate to the rest of him. His face is covered in a molded plastic mask shaped into a monstrous green visage, and he wears a nylon body suit painted to match, with bat-like vinyl wings attached to the back. The chin visible under the mask belongs to an older man, one with as many scars as his taller counterparts.

Over the gimmick suit he wears a street-battered leather jacket with holes surgically cut into it through which his wings fit comfortably, as if he simply hasn't bothered to change out of his gear after the last show.

He's a mini, the cherished and popular variety of little person wrestlers who often accompany their rudo or técnico counterparts to the ring, as well as entertain the crowd in their own matches.

"Goblin!" Cal shouts with equal parts surprise and pleasure. "Goblin, Junior! The baddest mini any rudo ever had as his minion! I didn't think you'd still be in town!"

The little man sprints to the bar, and Cal slaps him on his slight shoulder.

"I never thought you'd come back," Goblin laments. "I never thought you *could* come back."

"I'm not here to *work*," Cal assures him heavily. "In the ring or out of it. A Calavera honors his word of life, and death."

"Oh. Right." There's obvious disappointment in Goblin's voice.

"It's been that bad, eh?" Cal asks.

The grizzled veteran mini shrugs. "It wasn't so bad after you blew town. I mean, obviously it was bad," he says quickly. "I was wrecked, you having to leave. But a vato has to earn a living, you know? I signed on with Satanico Incorporated. We had a good run for a while, until they got signed in Japan and left me behind. After that I traded down from mid-card to curtain jerking. These last few years have been rough. All over. Not a lot of real rudos left, you ask me. These days you're more likely to get gunned down in Li'l Zee by an Otomies drive-by. They don't respect shit."

"Otomies?"

"Street gang. One minute they were just some tags on a bridge or on a storefront gate, next thing you know they were everywhere. They're cartel errand boys. Money must've grown them fast. No respect for enmascarados, even the baddest rudos on the block."

Cal orders them a couple of drinks and they both settle onto barstools.

"I'm sorry, buddy," Cal says sincerely. "Do you need a little help?"

He reaches inside his jacket and removes a skull money clip with a thick wad of bills clinched between its jaws.

Goblin reaches up and pushes it away.

"I ain't no charity case, Jefe," he insists. "If you got work for me I'm there, but I don't want no hand-outs. You can buy me another three or four drinks, though."

Calavera does, and they spend the next hour knocking them back and catching up on old times.

"I miss the gold, Jefe," Goblin drunkenly laments after just the second round. "I miss the gold belts we stole in the ring, and the gold bricks we took out of all those vaults and armored cars."

Calavera nods solemnly, taking a sip and a puff of his cigar.

Goblin's eyes, glassy from drink, suddenly light up "Hey. Hey! You remember when you lured that puto El Victor into the abandoned mineshaft?"

Cal laughs immediately. "Simón que sí. He thought it was my secret lair, but it was really just a pit infested with rabid badgers."

"No, no!" Goblin insists. "The other mineshaft. The one he thought we were keeping those kidnapped cheerleaders in, but instead we flooded it with all that sewer waste from the trailer park!"

Cal laughs even harder as Goblin rolls on. "And then the time he fell into that big cavern, and we dropped all those little kid department store dummies on him dressed like me! He thought they were real goblins!"

Cal has to steady Goblin by the shoulder as he laughs so hard he almost falls from his stool.

"That was so good. Mi dios...oh..."

Eventually the laughter tapers off, as does the reminiscing. Though Cal would never tell his former minion, he's glad when the small man runs out of memories and half-baked tales.

The truth is remembering the past and what he was forced to give up causes Cal more pain than a hundred chair shots.

When it's time for them to pack it in, Cal leaves a hundred-dollar tip for the old bartender and slips several more inside the lining of Goblin's leather, despite the little man's protests.

"One last thing," Cal says. "Where're things at with my art fencing operation? Did anyone step in after me? Try to muscle control?"

Goblin shakes his head.

"No one filled that hole, Jefe. High-end art ain't exactly knocking over a truck. No one with your skills or connections around. Why? Is that why you came here? You thinkin' about taking the reins back?"

Cal shrugs. "I'm just a naturally curious vato. You know that."

He grins and winks at his longtime associate.

"See you around, amigo," he says, gripping Goblin by the shoulder.

When Calavera hits the street the temperature has dropped over twenty degrees from when he entered the bar.

Rencor is still too close to the desert winds, Cal thinks, cinching his custom blazer and walking up the street.

He started to feel it on the back of his neck as soon as he exited the bar, but it's two more blocks before the feeling takes hold of him completely.

It isn't the cold. It's his natural radar for danger.

You wouldn't notice any visible change in his posture, gait, or expression, but inside Calavera is suddenly working at five times capacity, his peripheral vision scouting every dark corner and his mind formulating a dozen plans.

On the next block Calavera seemingly wanders from the street down a blind, dead-end alley. He stops several yards down its length and removes a cigar, clipping it and lighting it on his lips.

He takes a deep drag, turning to the opening of the alley. Cal exhales, sliding his other hand in his pocket and flicking ash, waiting.

Three of them enter the alley, rounding both corners coming from both ends of the street beyond.

They must have been waiting to cut him off, trapping Calavera between them.

They're all young Latinos with hard faces and the questionable facial hair grooming of youth, punks wearing the same gang colors. Each one is clad in a leather vest with tribal tableaus spray-painted on them. The most prominent marking is a jagged-edged rendering of a map of Mexico with an "O" painted on it.

The biggest one has an "88" shaved into the side of his skull.

Cal puffs on his cigar, unperturbed. "You must be the Otomies. I was just speaking with a colleague of mine about your fine organization."

"¿Qué pasa, abuelito?" 88 asks him with open hostility. "What'choo want around here?"

"Oh, mijo. I think you know exactly who I am and exactly what I want. You were waiting for me outside the bar. Word still spreads fast around here, eh?"

In response 88 whips out a butterfly knife and deploys its concealed blade with a flourish. "We don't need has-beens like you coming into the hood and stirring up all these old masks, making them think they matter again. This barrio is ours now."

Cal nods slowly, taking another few puffs of cigar.

"Rule of the jungle," he agrees, amiably. "It's yours as long as you can hold it."

"Just get the fuck out of Li'l Zee and Rencor, or we're going to show your ass some pain."

"Mijo, you don't know pain," Cal assures him, his tone dark and serious. "Not at that place under the skin. Not like an enmascarado does. Let me show you."

Cal raises his arm, empty palm up and lain bare in front of them.

His other hand suddenly stubs out his own cigar in the middle of that palm's flesh, grinding the burning end deep.

Cal never flinches through his mask.

"What the fuck?"

"¡Soy loco, man!"

Cal clinches his fist around the ashes and still-burning ember.

With their attention all focused on his hand, Cal introduces 88 to one of his favorite old wrestling maneuvers: a sudden, swift, devastating kick to the groin.

88's eyes go crossed and his whole body attempts to fold inward like a collapsing star. Then Cal closes his smoldering hand and launches a fist with inhuman speed into the mouth and chin of 88, knocking his body onto the concrete, the impact sending the knife flying from his hand.

Closed fists and nut shots are the first two chapters in the rudo playbook, the ones heroes are forbidden to read, and Calavera just closed the book on the gangbanger.

One of the other Otomies goes for a pistol stuck in his waistband. Cal reaches out and grabs his wrist, halting his gun hand. In almost the same motion, he head-butts him in the face and knocks him down too. The third one falls on him and there's a brief struggle, but in less than three seconds Cal has pulled the punk across his shoulders and is lifting his entire body in the air, spinning it around before ramming the Otomi's head into the side of a dumpster and pitching him to the ground.

Airplane spins are a técnico trademark, but it takes a rudo to add ramming your opponent's head into a dumpster.

Calavera stands over the fallen gangbangers, his feet spread and knees bent in a fighting stance, hands held raised and ready in front of him.

The thrill is almost overwhelming; all the years of standing in the background, watching people like Stella take down the villains he set up for them. Oh, there was the occasional intimidating of a suspect, but real combat is something he hasn't seen in over five years, not since the waning days of his wrestling career after leaving Rencor. Blood pumps thunderously through his heart, and there's an intense, satisfying heat emanating from his groin.

Unfortunately, in his excitement he's forgotten the nature of street gangs. They're a lot like ants. You never see just one.

You certainly never see three attacking all alone.

In the next moment the opening of the alley is filled with five more bodies clad in Otomies gang colors. More drop into the alley from the walls of the buildings. They drop over the fence dead-ending the alley. They emerge from every crevasse like flesh-eating bacteria overwhelming its host from within.

There's no more banter. Cal lets out a savage war cry as they converge on him. He manages to take down the first few before it becomes a swarm and his limbs are literally weighted down and neutralized by the mass of bodies surging over and around him. Fists and the soles of shoes rain down on him from everywhere. His wrestling instincts kick in and he covers up as best he can, protecting his most vulnerable areas, but the pummeling is intense.

What seems to him like an eternity later, Cal finds himself kneeling on the filthy alley floor with three Otomies restraining his arms and head.

88, blood bubbling on his lips and trying to straighten his dislocated jaw, stands over him.

"Bleed him, carnal!" one of the others bids 88.

"Nah. Nah. I always wanted to do this."

88 reaches out and grabs a handful of Calavera's mask.

Cal struggles like a trapped animal, but he's held tight.

88 yanks the mask side-to-side roughly and then rips it off his head.

The rest of the gang gasps collectively.

Underneath his mask, Cal is wearing another mask.

It's the same iconic skull, only this one is silver and gold.

He grins up at 88 and spits blood at the gang leader.

"¡Chingon!" 88 growls, striking him in the cheek.

He reaches out with both hands and rips Cal's mask off again.

He finds a third beneath it, purple and pink this time.

Now Cal is laughing.

"Fuck it!" 88 growls, taking up his knife again. "Let's just do this!"

Cal should be focused on the knife about to open his flesh, but he's not. His keen eyes are focused over and far past the right shoulder of 88, staring at one of the fire escapes on the side of the building above them.

He's suddenly as surprised as the Otomies trying to unmask him.

With a yell of "¡Victoria!" that draws every eye in the alley, El Victor leaps from the fire escape, arms wide in a twenty-foot suicide dive. He falls on five of the gangbangers in front of Cal at once like a curse from Heaven itself, knocking them down as easily as bowling pins.

The Otomies holding Cal loosen their grip and let their attention flag just enough. Cal jerks his arm free and elbows one of them in the groin, punching the thug holding his other arm right in the breadbasket. Reaching up, he grabs the punk's neck and snap-mares him onto his back, then grabs the ankles of the one holding him by the neck and yanks the kid's feet out from under him furiously.

In a moment he's back on his feet, and what happens next is the wet-dream-come-true of every diehard lucha fan in Rencor and around the world, even if none of them will ever get to see it happen.

El Victor III and El Mil Calaveras III are standing back-to-back, fighting the same battle, *together*.

In three generations of the men in their family donning their respective hoods, no Victor or Calavera has ever fought beside the other.

They...THEY...*La pareja increíble*...begin to clear the alley with the skill and instincts born of decades brawling in and around rings on five continents, Victor fighting with the restrained, old school etiquette and guts of a técnico while Cal kicks, punches, and gnaws on the skull of anything that comes near him.

"You!" a bloodied and battered 88 calls to Calavera from across the alley.

Cal levels the gangbanger he's grappling with by driving an elbow into the back of his head. He turns to face their leader, poised, even eager for the punk to take another run at him.

88 strides across the alley, fist cocked, but before he can close the gap between him and Calavera, Victor intercedes, tackling the thug and wrapping his arms around 88's waist, hoisting him into the air and onto his right shoulder.

Cal has seen this move a thousand times, though mostly in replays featuring himself being devastated by it. Victor is about to deliver The Victory Spike to 88, his family's famous finishing maneuver, a cross between a tombstone piledriver and powerbomb that spikes an opponent on his shoulders with atomic force.

Cal feels a sudden surge of fury and affront at Victor snapping off his prey, let alone using the move that ended so many of their matches, right in front of him.

Before Victor can tilt 88's body forward and execute the Victory Spike, Cal reaches out and loops his arm around the thug's head, placing the grip on him that precedes the Calaveras' own family finishing move, The Skull Crusher. He locks eyes with Victor over the gangbanger's helpless form, Cal's gaze challenging. He's put Victor away as many times with the family's patented inverted bulldog as Victor has spiked him for the win.

Instead of either of them putting 88 away, however, they're suddenly engaged in a human tug-of-war for control of the helpless thug. It ends with all three of their bodies collapsing to the ground in an embarrassing heap.

Both Calavera and Victor curse each other around the groaning gang leader's body.

Several of the Otomies who have recovered from their decking by Victor converge on them both, forcing Victor to redirect his anger with Calavera into a final assault on the Otomies. He fights to his feet and begins pummeling them with forearms and knees to the body.

Amidst the chaos, Calavera throws an armbar on 88 and snaps the limb that earlier threatened him with the knife.

The thug's scream is like music to his ears.

Less than sixty seconds later the Otomies realize discretion is the better part of valor. As the final banger escapes the alley, Victor and Calavera stand almost shoulder-to-shoulder, panting each breath, their bodies tense from the fight as they watch their enemies flee before them with satisfaction.

Their enemies...

The enmascarados turn towards each other.

Their eyes peer through the holes of their respective hoods.

Realization hits them like cold water as they face each other like gunslingers at high noon.

"I didn't believe it," Victor says, and the tone of his voice backs him up. "I saw you with my own eyes, and I still didn't believe it. Even from you. Even after everything you did, to me and to everyone else. I didn't believe you'd break *that* rule. I didn't think you could live with yourself if you *came back*."

"I guess you stopped doing your job, hero," Cal responds coldly. "So they called me in to do it for you."

Nothing about his words computes for Victor. "What does that mean?"

Cal grins the same bloody grin Victor has stared at in hundreds of matches.

"You haven't heard? I work for the good guys now, helping them catch top-of-the-food-chain desperados like...*me*...or like I was, anyway."

Victor isn't able to answer right away.

"You're lying," he finally manages. "It's a lie. Another trick."

"Check it out for yourself!" Victor snaps. "The FBI is here investigating the museum heist. I'm supposed to profile the thieves."

"*You're* the thief!"

"Nope. Sorry Vic. Was in Chicago. Ask Stella."

"No way! Even if the FBI was crazy enough to hire you...there's no way you didn't take the job *just to get yourself back to Rencor.*"

At that, Calavera's face suddenly drops.

Even through his mask he looks shocked. More than that, he looks aghast, genuinely taken aback by Victor's words.

His tense fighting stance goes slack, and he almost stumbles around the stupefied Victor, walking past him and stopping to stare at the alley wall.

"I never thought of that," he finally says, his voice as stunned as his expression.

"What are you talking about?" Vic demands.

"Five years working with those bastards...it never even occurred to me to stage a crime here so they'd send me back. It's brilliant! It's perfect! And I...never...once...thought of it!"

He sounds utterly sincere, even heartbroken by the revelation.

Victor can't believe it.

Cal looks back at him in abject horror. "How could you...*you*...think of a plan like that, and I didn't?"

Victor just shakes his head, at a loss.

They're interrupted by loud footfalls and rising voices.

Half-a-dozen rudos from the bar are suddenly filtering into the alley, their voices questioning.

All of them lay eyes on Victor at the same time.

"El Victor!"

"I don't believe it!"

"In Li'l Zee!"

"The balls!"

"He put my cousin away."

"He put *me* away!"

"Persecuting enmascarados just to keep himself in the papers!"

"LET'S KILL HIM!"

A wave of masked men surge forward.

Calavera halts them.

He steps in-between the mob of rudos and Victor, holding up his burnt, bloody hand in warning.

"No one touches him!" Cal insists.

The others stop, staring at him in shock.

"He did you the worst, Calavera!"

"No one touches him *but me*," Cal amends his statement. "He's going to walk out of Li'l Zee on his own two feet because I'm going to be the one to break his legs. ¿Comprende?"

Even if they wanted to, not a single one of them would question Calavera.

Cal turns back to Victor.

"You owe me one, hero," he whispers.

"You messed up your suit," is all Victor says in return.

"Is that the same ring jacket from ten years ago? Seriously, Victor? Nice jeans, too."

Cal leaves him standing there, speechless and steaming, as he ushers the others back up the alley, but he does indeed look down and examine the damage done to his fine tailoring.

MIDNIGHT MOVIES

Stella doesn't sleep much, averaging four hours on the best of nights. She's never learned to shut her brain down; to let go of the case, her career and the many related woes, the burden of her current charge, namely a genuine former super villain. The hamster is always on the wheel in Stella's head, and that's what makes her good at her job and bad at everything else.

The Bureau has put her and Cal up at the Azteca Suites in Rencor's revitalized downtown commerce district. She has her own room with double beds, one of which is currently occupied by an empty pizza box. She took it down all by herself earlier in the night.

She may be five-foot-five with the mass of a cherry tree, but her metabolism is Olympian and she eats with the same competitive spirit.

Stella sits on the opposite bed in a Hartford Whalers jersey and jeans, watching an old monster movie from the late 50's on the room's television. She recognizes the hero of the grainy black-and-white film, a masked man battling some poor stuntman in a clunky robot costume; it's El Victor, the first one, grandfather of the man who ended Calavera's wrestling career.

Though she's no wrestling fan, Stella has poured through Calavera's file diligently.

Stella flips to another channel and blinks, confused. It's another El Victor movie. The entire look of this film, however, is different. It's in color, but looks cheaper somehow, less accomplished, and the tone of the content strikes her as sillier and sleazier. Victor is fighting what look like a cross between a Satanic biker gang and Chinese monks. And there's a half-naked woman chained up in the background. Several, actually.

She realizes this must be a movie from the later 1970's, which means that's not the original El Victor; it's the second one, the father of Cal's old "nemesis."

Stella rolls her eyes.

Jesus, she thinks, television here is like the 24-hour Victor network.

And how does anyone keep them straight?

She changes the channel again, relieved to not see a red-and-white masked man.

Her relief doesn't last long.

After a home-movie-looking shot of an apparently well-known local singer exiting a nightclub with his girlfriend, Stella finds herself looking at an even more pixelated, long distance shot of herself and Cal at Rencor's Airfield.

A logo in the corner of the screen reads "Rencor Insider."

A gossip-mongering voiceover informs the audience: "But the *biggest* news of the day, is this a legendary rudo once thought banished forever in a classic Loser-Leaves-Town match at the Coliseo *returning* to Rencor? Our unconfirmed reports say—"

"Well, so much for a *low-profile* operation!" Stella leans forward and shouts at the screen.

She's about to launch into a tirade of cursing when the show gives way to a commercial break, and the first ad stops her dead.

Two elderly masked men, one decrepit and ancient and the other a still-virile mid-sixties, stand behind a desk in matching royal purple suits. Their hoods are the same design as Cal's, the geezer's a simple black and white leather deal that looks as old as he does, and the other more like Cal's but with less intricate color and flare. They're standing on what is obviously a cheap cardboard set made up to look like an office, complete with rows of fake plastic book spines behind them.

"Rencor rudos," the younger of them addresses the camera mechanically, "have you been swerved by a lawsuit from some fan you justifiably slapped on your way to the ring?"

The ancient enmascarado takes over in a voice that sounds like a scratched up Victrola recording: "Did you have no other choice but to snatch the chancla from the hand of some abuela at ringside and give her the business end of it?"

Using an imaginary sandal, he weakly mimics striking the old woman in question.

"Or were you left high and dry by un-loyal henchman in a poorly planned heist...ALLEGEDLY?" his younger counterpart continues. "If so, call Calavera y Calavera, Attorneys-at-Law. We come to the rudo's rescue!"

"And no técnico ever makes the rap stick when we are your pick!" the eldest Calavera adds, almost falling over the desk in front of them.

His son steadies him.

"1-800-RUDO-RESCUE" flashes at the bottom of the screen like some graphic from 1980's television.

"Where...the hell...am I?" Stella marvels.

Someone knocks with a heavy fist at her door.

Stella uses the remote to quickly change the channel and mute the screen. She checks the time on her phone, seeing that it's past 2:00 in the morning.

Her brow furrows at the closed door.

Retrieving her sidearm from the drawer of the nightstand, she stands and approaches the door to her room cautiously.

"Who is it?"

Through the door: "Booty call, Señorita."

Stella frowns, recognizing the voice immediately. She relaxes her grip on her pistol and opens the door.

Cal has cleaned himself up after the evening's excitement. He's wearing a garish leopard-print smoking jacket with black lapels and, of course, a skull monogram. He's holding a lit cigar in one hand, which also cradles a martini with three olives, and a second martini in the other hand.

"This is a non-smoking room," Stella informs him immediately.

Cal shrugs, closing the door behind him with an elbow. "I'm the bad guy. What do you want?"

Stella's frown deepens. "For you to remember you're reformed."

"That's why I have you—" he begins, but stops as his eyes catch the silent images of Victor II on the television screen. "For real? For *real*? This is what you're watching?"

"What? It's the middle of the night and it's the only thing on!"

Calavera stares at the television's screen for several moments. He picks up the remote and changes the channel only to find yet another El Victor movie playing.

"¡Putos!" he exclaims.

"I kind of like this one, actually, check out that huge robot..."

"*Why*?" Cal demands, appalled.

Stella shrugs. "What? It reminds me of Creature Double Feature on Channel 56 back home when I was a kid. They ran two crappy movies like this every Saturday." She pauses. "Hey, were you ever in any of—"

"No."

"No movies? Your father or your grandfather, then? They were popular. Or did they just do cheesy lawyer commercials?"

"...no."

"Why not?"

"They don't...they didn't put rudos in these movies. We don't get film franchises."

"Why?"

Cal snorts. "We'd steal all the heat from these clowns," he insists, puffing on his cigar and sipping his martini.

Stella picks up the remote and kills the image on the TV. "So, what did you get up to out there tonight? No old tricks, I trust."

"Just...re-acclimating to a hostile environment."

"Yeah? You turn up any leads for us."

Cal waves his cigar-cradling hand at her dismissively. "*Leads.* This is still my town. I'll find out who knocked over the museum in five minutes tomorrow."

"Tomorrow we're having the meeting we were *supposed* to have today with local PD to discuss this case."

"There's nothing to discuss."

"Then it'll be a short meeting."

"Cops in Rencor couldn't find their own culo with a GPS. The only real crime busters in this city were luchadores. Even though it doesn't look like they're doing much of that kind of business anymore, we should meet with Medianoche anyway. The old gordo is the last enmascarado in this city still doing real hero work. Consider it unspoken protocol."

"Actually, we *don't* need to meet with him. I read about your 'heroes' and their weird-ass consulting or auxiliary program or whatever it was while I was prepping for this assignment. A Captain...Bustamante? I think? He shuttered the program on orders from the city council a few weeks ago."

Calavera just blinks through his mask at first, legitimately taken aback by the news.

"Well. Then it's...Bustamante. I remember him."

Stella sighs. "He better back us up. I don't want to be here any longer than we have to."

Calavera doesn't say anything to that.

"Cal?" Stella probes.

"What?"

"Is this going to be a problem? Working here?"

"For who?"

"If it's a problem for you then you become a problem for me, and I don't need any more of those, not with the Bureau."

"That's not my fault. You got yourself here."

"Don't remind me," Stella grumbles, returning to sit on her bed.

"Don't worry," Cal says, an uncustomary sympathetic tone in his voice. "I'll make you look so good on this one you'll be back in your bosses' good graces in no time."

"I'll believe it when I see it. I need you on your best behavior. It was more bullshit than I ever thought it would be, getting you cleared to work here on this case. I thought that whole 'Loser-Leaves-Town' thing was just, y'know, schtick. Did you know it's actually *legislated*? It's a statute in the old city codes."

Cal shrugs, staring down at her like a child explaining two plus two equals four to an adult.

"Of course," he says simply.

"But that's ridiculous! It's medieval! It's like this place is a pre-Magna Carta fiefdom or something."

"It's a lucha libre town. It was built around wrestling, for wrestling. Wrestling regulations and the law are the same thing in Rencor. That's why I had to break both so often."

"Tell me about it. I had to call in the last favors I had to get you a temporary reprieve. And it expires quickly, so we need to put this thing to bed."

"We will. I promise."

"Good." She looks up at him as he casually sips his martini.

"What else do you need?" she asks.

Cal shrugs. "I'm a villain, but I'm still a gentleman. I'm waiting to be invited to sit."

"Then consider yourself invited, provided you return to your own room."

"Aw, c'mon now—"

"I have a gun."

Cal holds up his encumbered hands. "Like I said, I'm a gentleman. I only need to be told once."

"Every few weeks, it seems."

"I've taken a lot of shots to the head," he says as he places the second martini on a side table by the door for her. "Sue me."

He opens the door and lets it trail shut behind him after he exits.

Stella shakes her head, grinning.

She tries never to grin like that in front of Calavera.

It would only encourage him.

THE ODD COUPLE SWERVE

"I always wondered what happened to him after he left the city," Gypsy says with awe. "Didn't you ever wonder what happened to him?"

"I assumed he hung himself in a dirty motel room in Tijuana."

Gypsy's face registers genuine shock. "Victor!"

Victor stretches the cloth around his mouth into a frown. "I'm sorry. You're right. That was way too dark."

The first thing Victor notices when he enters the squad room is the lithe blond leaning against a desk, wearing FBI credentials and a suit that sets her even further apart from the off-the-rack, style deficient city detectives surrounding her. She was the one in the squad room when he first spotted his old enemy back in town, the one Calavera high-tailed it with after their brief brawl.

She spots him, as well, keying in on his red and white "V" mask immediately.

"Nice to see you again," Stella says, as if staring at him under a microscope. "We didn't actually get to meet the first time. You're El Victor. I watched two generations of your family fighting robot bikers on TV last night."

"You're correct, ma'am," Vic confirms easily, unshaken, having been identified this way countless times. "Except about the robot bikers. That never happened. Although it would've been a great flick."

"You're right. It was a robot and then bikers. Satanic bikers."

Victor nods.

She offers him her hand, a curious look on her face Victor can't quite identify.

"I'm Special Agent Stella O'Shaughnessy, Federal Bureau of Investigations."

Victor shakes it gently.

"I must apologize for my behavior here before. I was...overcome. I didn't realize...the situation."

"I noticed," Stella says, suppressing a grin.

"May I introduce you to the good doctor here, Gitana Jimenez, my personal physician."

"You can call me Gypsy," she says, offering Stella her hand.

The Special Agent is obviously dubious of Victor's "personal physician" claim, but she shakes Gypsy's hand just the same.

"I assume the Bureau is here because of the museum robbery," Victor says.

Stella nods. "I'm in charge of an...asset...that specializes in art and artifact theft — are you okay?"

In the middle of her sentence Victor's eyes have developed a removed, increasingly angry look.

They're staring over her shoulder.

Inside the glass cube of Captain Bustamante's office, Gus is staring across his desk at Calavera, who's reclining in one of the guest chairs with his booted, skull-heeled feet on the desk.

"Yes, ma'am. It's your...*asset* I need to talk to Captain Bustamante about. Excuse me," he manages tightly before moving past Stella.

Victor storms inside the office, slamming the door behind him.

"You can't be serious!" he fires at Gus without preamble.

"It's good to see you too, Vic," the Captain offers amiably.

"He's a public menace!" Victor thunders. "He terrorized this city for years!"

"Most of that was in the ring and perfectly legal," Cal insists.

"And his family terrorized my family! They kidnapped my mother multiple, *multiple* times!"

"She understood how the business works. It was for publicity! She once made me and my henchmen coffee while we waited for you."

"She didn't make you coffee!"

"With egg shells. Old school. Never had better. Hmm...I bet she's still *fine*, too"

Behind his desk, Gus chokes on nothing more than the air he's breathing after that comment.

"I should beat you to death with your own ridiculous boots for even saying that to me!"

"Not in my office," Gus insists. "And those aren't the words of a hero, Victor."

"He's a *criminal*! The only reason he isn't behind bars is his double-talking lawyer papá."

"I defended *myself* after I got my law degree," Cal insists, feigning hurt feelings.

"He cut holes in the vault floors of the bank, like 18 times!"

"But there was never proof I actually *stole* anything. And I did six months for breaking and entering...once."

"He heisted every single piece of fine art that ever came through Rencor! Half of which was never even recovered!"

"Well now you're just being silly, Victor. I couldn't possibly have done all of that and have a job at the FBI, could I? The good guys don't work like that."

Chuckling, Cal holds up his hands innocently to punctuate the statement, looking over at Gus like a problem child determined to con the school principal out of punishing him.

It's obvious Vic wants to start using words the hero code he was raised with since birth forbids him to use in a public setting.

Behind his desk, Gus is grinning ear-to-ear.

"This isn't funny, Gus," Victor chastises him.

"No, it's not," the Captain admits. "But I believe it's...it's needed."

"What does that mean?" Victor demands.

Gus sighs. "Victor, you're right. Calavera is too dangerous and has too violent a history in this city to be allowed to run around unchecked, even with his FBI escort. I don't know that woman. The citizenry of Rencor doesn't, either. And this city isn't big on trusting outsiders. This won't work."

Calavera sighs.

Victor claps his hands together in triumph. "Thank you!"

"That's why I want you to work *with him* on this case, Victor" Gus says. "You can keep an eye on him through all of this."

Cal grins. "Nice swerve, Bus."

"Do *not* call me that!" the Captain hurls back, suddenly dead serious.

"Gus, you have to be out of your mind! Técnicos don't work with rudos! You're asking a mongoose to partner with a cobra."

"He's not a rudo anymore," Gus corrects him. "He's on our side. And he's not a luchador anymore, either."

Neither of them notices Cal's eyes dropping beneath his hood at that.

"I won't do it," Victor says resolutely. "My father would disown me, and my grandfather would literally kill me."

"That's one thing we have in common," Cal mutters.

"Fine!" Gus proclaims. "Don't tell me, though. Tell him."

The Captain flicks his chin at the window facing out from his office. Both Vic and Cal turn to look.

Standing in the squad room beyond, currently grilling a very annoyed Stella, is an out-of-place-looking man in a rumpled suit with a weasel face belied by intensely sharp, intelligent blue eyes. He's holding up a smartphone, the screen of which currently shows an image of an old-fashioned tape recorder's face.

The tape recorder is running.

"Cortez," Victor whispers in disbelief. Then, his voice rising: "You called the biggest dirt-slinging reporter in this whole city?"

"This case is big news, Vic. And it's the kind of news we don't get much of any more. It's the kind of news that doesn't involve drugs or blood or kidnappings. It's a story about *a caper*, not a crime, something folks can follow and not be afraid of. It's a story that gets their blood up, but doesn't make them afraid to walk the streets. People want that. They need it. And when I told him there were enmascarados involved? Just like the old days? He frothed at the mouth, practically."

"That's low, Gus," Victor judges him.

"That's brilliant," Cal adds. "And...some press could help flush out our quarry."

Gus gives Cal a surprised nod, then fixes Victor with a deep stare. "You want to go out there and tell Cortez and everyone in this city that El Victor isn't answering Rencor's call for help, be my guest."

"Why? Why are you doing this?" Victor asks, and he suddenly sounds more curious than angry.

Gus looks at Calavera, as if he doesn't want to say his next words in front of the famous villain.

In the end, he sighs and lets it loose: "Because I had to fire one of my heroes recently. Because you walking out on this department years back was a big mistake, for you and for us. Because I think the two of you doing this can help the city...way beyond recovering some stolen relics. Plus..."

He silently mouths "...REANIMATED MUMMY!" at Vic, childlike enthusiasm overcoming him.

Victor seems stuck, unsure of how to respond.

But he's no longer protesting.

"If I might interject," Cal speaks up. "Those all may be good reasons for *him*. But I don't give two pesos what the people in this city think or feel. What's in this for me?"

"Your cushy FBI profiling gig depends on it," Gus says flatly.

Gus looks to Victor. "Excuse us for just a moment, all right? Just do whatever your heart tells you is right. That's all a hero can ever do."

Calavera rolls his eyes and reaches into his jacket for a cigar.

"You light that thing in here and I'll shoot you myself," Gus says automatically.

Victor walks to the door and grasps the handle, steeling himself before he walks out into the squad room.

Cortez and the reporter's recording app meet him.

"El Victor! We have reports of a mummy stalking our city streets. It's exactly the kind of mystery that was the specialty of your family in the old days. Are you coming out of retirement as a crimefighter in Rencor's hour of need?"

Victor takes a deep breath, his eyes sliding past the reporter to regard Gypsy standing on the other side of the room.

With unflinchingly hopeful eyes, she gives him the slightest of nods.

"All I can say," Victor speaks for the man's recording app, "is that for three generations my family has battled the evils plaguing Rencor in and out of the ring, and I won't be the Victor to break from that legacy. That's all the comment I have right now."

"What about the return of Calavera? Is he your prime suspect?"

As if on cue, Cal emerges from Gus's office, straightening his tie delicately.

"On the contrary," he announces to Cortez. "I'm part of the solution to this problem. Isn't that right, Victor? Meet Rencor PD's new secret weapon."

Cortez looks like his head is about to explode. "Wait...you two... you're—"

"On the same case," Victor says through clenched teeth. "Technically."

Cal beams at his reaction.

"El Mil Calaveras!" Cortez shouts at him as if he's trying to speak above a legion of other reporters, despite being the only one in the room. "You were banished from Rencor by El Victor. Why would you agree to work alongside him? Is this a classic Calavera double-cross in the making?"

Cal grins. "I certainly wouldn't tell you if it was."

"Then why? Why cross the line drawn in blood and preserved by three generations of both your clans?"

"Because there's a rumor something nastier than me is walking the streets of my city. And if they're true I owe it to my father and my grandfather to find it and take our title back from it. Even if that means doing the unthinkable."

Victor looks back at Gus, who is now standing beside Stella, watching the scene unfold.

Glancing down at her as if suddenly noticing she's there, Gus abruptly sucks in his gut as well as he can, tugging up his pants by the belt.

Stella pretends not to notice, but she grins, looking up at him. "You know, I've always been a big fan of Mexican."

Gus nearly loses control over his straining gut. "I...excuse me?"

"Food," she says. "Mexican food."

"Oh. Uh. Right. Of course. Who isn't?"

She scans her eyes over him appraisingly. "I bet you know some great places."

Gus looks down at her, at first thinking she's making a joke about his weight, but then realizing that's not what her eyes and posture are trying to tell him at all.

In fact, the message is just the opposite.

The surprise stifles him for a few moments, but then he slowly begins returning her grin.

Meanwhile, Cortez closes down his recording app, practically beaming. "That's great shit, you guys. I can't believe I'm standing here watching this. *¡La Pareja Increíble!* You should feel my nipples right now."

"You're still all class, Cortez," Victor says dryly. "Are your mummy sightings for real?"

Cortez shrugs. "Shambling guy in stinking bandages, spotted by at least half-a-dozen unnamed witnesses. As real as any story of mine ever gets."

"That's all you've got?" Victor presses.

"That's all we need," Calavera assures him. "And I know where to start."

PART THREE

PAREJAS

MOLE & SAUSAGE

Calavera has been standing across the street from Coliseo Rencor staring up at the decrepit yet somehow beautiful structure for almost two full minutes.

Standing beside him, Victor watches the rudo, growing impatient, but on a preternatural level understanding exactly what Cal is feeling in this moment. He's like an exiled priest returning to the church of his excommunication.

He's also like a soldier returning home after a long war. A war he lost.

The arena is both of those things to the wrestlers, particularly the champions, for whom its ring is their primary battlefield and its locker rooms their sanctuary.

"I've got an informant to see," Victor reminds him.

"Me too," Cal answers, distracted.

"We're not actually going in, you know," Victor offers.

"I know."

"Because you *can't* go in."

"I *know*, and I don't need you to remind me. Puto. But I can smell the bacon and the hot dogs from out here."

"So can you finish soaking it in and let's get on the case?"

Cal looks over at him, danger flashing in his eyes.

"Don't think anything is settled between us," he says. "I may need to keep up appearances for this gig, but I haven't forgotten who took my city away from me, and I never will."

"If you want to settle it we can do it right now!"

"I don't need to beat you here anymore than I already have!" Cal fires back. "You know I'm ahead in lifetime falls at the arena between us, right?"

"...bullshit."

"Sixty-three to sixty-one in the Coliseo, my favor. I checked the records. About a thousand times in the last ten years."

"Well then it's too bad you couldn't win the one that counted."

"I had the flu that weekend."

Victor actually takes a step back, as if a steel gauntlet has just slapped him.

It's somehow a worse insult than anything Cal has ever leveled at him.

Calavera's hard stare doesn't waver.

"Take it back," Victor insists.

"No."

"Take it back! Take it back now!"

"No!"

Victor steps close and Calavera puffs out his chest, the two men's masks almost forehead to forehead.

Victor is practically shaking, itching to strike.

But he doesn't.

"You go see your informant and I'll go see mine," he manages through grinding teeth.

"Fine."

They part ways, but never take eyes off each other.

Victor walks across the street, bearing right, around the arena's arched circumference, while Cal takes the same path but to the left. The smell of the bacon-wrapped hot dogs is maddening, and he's suddenly forgotten all about the case they're supposed to be investigating.

He just wants a 'dogo.'

Calavera wanders around the perimeter of the arena, hoping to catch the old man with his improvised shopping cart grille, or the son that has probably replaced him in the last decade.

When he gets to the back of the circular building though, he happens upon a different kind of wiener.

An aged, muddled-brown dog trots up to Calavera and begins sniffing excitedly around his left shoe and ankle.

Cal crouches down, stroking the tiny, elongated dog's head, which is covered in a miniature luchador's mask striped like a court jester's hat, complete with attached bells.

"Chorizo!" Calavera greets the canine. "How the hell are you still alive?"

"How do you know Chorizo?"

It's Victor, having come full-circle from the opposite direction, standing in front of them, looking down at the pair in total confusion.

Cal's tone mirrors his rival's when he asks back, "How do *you* know Chorizo?"

"Wait. Your informant is Topo? Your snitch is Topo?"

"You know Topo, too?"

"Topo is *my* informant," Victor insists.

Calavera stands, staring daggers back at him.

"No, Topo was part of my network. How do you think I stayed one step ahead of you so many times?"

"How do you think I always foiled you at the end of the day?"

Neither of them speaks for long contemplative moments after that.

Only a seasoned carnival barker voice from afar breaks the tense silence.

"Máscaras! Máaaaaascaras!!!"

At the same instant, Vic and Cal break into a heavy, fierce stride toward the source of the voice. Chorizo sprints to catch up, which he only does under yipping protest.

Topo is a short, perpetually hunched over man with a droopy face and an absurd mustache like a parody of a silent movie villain. He's holding the bottom end of towering ten-foot pole stretched high above his head, the shaft of which is totally obscured by the dozens and dozens of low-grade bootleg luchador masks hanging from it, fanned-out thicker toward the bottom, like a Technicolor Christmas tree. The cheap masks are *the* souvenir from a night at the arena, what lucha fans buy instead of t-shirts or foam fingers.

Vic and Cal approach the usual spot near the arena's back entrance the vendor/snitch uses as his 'office.'

"Topo!" Victor yells.

"You two-faced dirt merchant!" Calavera fumes.

Topo stares at one of them, then the other, back and forth for several seconds.

Though his sallow expression never changes, he's obviously either confused or concerned or some combination of both.

"This is weird, man."

"So, all those years, Topo?" Victor asks, not even trying to mask his hurt feelings over the matter. "You were playing me?"

Topo has a 'caught' look on his face, like a bad pet in the garbage as the kitchen light comes on, then shakes his head. "Not *playing*. I've got my own ethics. Every tip I gave you was always good. So was every tip I gave *him*." The last is said with a nod at Cal.

"That's not what 'ethics' means," Victor assures him.

Topo shrugs.

"Wait!" Cal interjects. "Just...wait. *You* were the one ratting me out to him?"

"Sí."

"Every time?"

"Sí."

Cal appears ready to explode.

"I should Huricanrana you into the pavement."

"No one's doing a number on anybody here," Victor insists.

"You don't tell me what to do, Boy Scout."

"I don't have to because you're one of the good guys now," Victor reminds him. "Remember? That's what you said to me."

"I kept a balanced book," Topo insists. "For every tip I give the técnico, I give one to the rudo. Like I said, ethics. What you doing back in town, Cal? And what you *two* doing together without throwing hands or chairs or something at each other's heads?"

"It's temporary," Victor assures him.

Cal takes a deep breath, speaking his next words begrudgingly: "We need to draw a bead on the smash-and-grab artists who drove that truck into the museum."

"And..." Victor adds, somewhat amazed at his own words, "we need to know if there's really a...*mummy*...wandering the city."

"I don't know nothing," Topo informs them.

"That's what you always say," Vic and Cal thunder in unison.

They look at each other, briefly, before returning their attention to the hunched-over snitch.

Topo sighs. "Buy a mask."

"You knew we were coming?" Victor blurts out.

Topo raises his tone a sly octave. *"Buy a mask..."*

"You're still pulling this shit?" Cal practically lunges at him.

Victor steadies him with one arm, which Cal bats away ferociously.

Topo only shrugs, flexing a finger repeatedly like an inchworm upward to the masks on the pole.

"Twenty bucks," he states firmly.

"TWENTY!" Cal spits. "They used to be ten! I'm going to tie you to the back of a fucking truck."

"¡Oye! We're in public, with that language!" Victor snaps at him.

Cal hangs his head. "I cannot believe this is happening. Any of this."

Victor reaches into the pocket of his ring jacket and produces a twenty-dollar bill.

Topo takes it and makes it disappear.

He reaches up his vertical bazaar, picks a certain red mask then changes his mind. Sifting higher up the pole, he eventually draws down a cheaply made copy of Calvera's mask and hands it to Victor with a slight chuckle.

"Let's get the hell out of here." Cal growls, turning.

"Ah-ah! Twenty bucks." Topo states sternly at the rudo, an expectant hand extended.

Cal stares daggers, but a stern look from Victor and a threatening growl from Chorizo persuade him out of whatever he was about to do. With a deflating exhalation he pulls a twenty from his skull-blazoned money clip and slaps it in Topo's hand.

Topo returns to the pole, to the same mask he nearly picked before, and hands it to the rudo.

It's a souvenir Victor hood.

This time he's unable to hide the chuckle.

"Enjoy..." the shady street vendor says, hobbling away.

Cal points a ringed finger at him. "This isn't over."

At Topo's feet, Chorizo's barks shrilly.

"Shut up!" Calavera snaps back at the wiener dog.

"Come on, man," Victor bids him.

Reluctantly, Calavera follows him away from the arena entrance.

"Ten years ago," Cal mutters to himself. "Ten years ago I would've hung him upside-down on the front of a speeding train."

"Come on, you...evidently...know the drill." he says, reaching inside the cheap mask and gesturing for Cal to do the same.

They each withdraw a small slip of paper with a few words scrawled in a shaky, poorly trained hand. They each read their papers, then show them to the other.

They *both* read: "Go get a new suit."

THE TAILOR

It's the only truly neutral ground for técnicos and rudos in Rencor. For decades an enmascarado's suit was his armor outside the wrestling ring, as signatory and sacred as a priest's cassock.

And in Rencor, there's still only one place to go for a true enmascarado looking to get fitted for a suit; that is, a suit laced with hidden elbow and knee guards, reinforced stitching and stretch zones tailored specifically for combat.

Lake Seco (referred to simply as "El Lago" by most of its residents) is a small pocket of steadily crumbling neighborhoods east of both downtown and Poquito Xibalba. Mostly removed from the chaos threading the streets of the rest of the city, it's populated largely by the elderly and what remains of the original founding families of the city, although not even they could tell you why it was named Lake Seco; there's never been a lake, dry or otherwise, only a small disused stone quarry that's mostly used as a breeding ground by teenagers.

The Tailor's shop occupies a small space above an old-fashioned chemist's in the heart of Lake Seco. There's no sign, only a heavy, blood red door at the top of a rickety exterior staircase.

Victor and Calavera are both silent as they make the short trek up those stairs, both recalling the times their fathers brought them here for their first suits.

Calavera was a punk himself then, wanting to wear leather jackets and studs outside the ring. It makes him laugh out loud, thinking of that kid and the man he became. Calavera rarely feels comfortable outside his suits now.

Victor, on the other hand, had wanted a suit like his father's ever since he could walk. It did, however, take him a decade to get comfortable in them, although not physically. It took him that long to feel he belonged in one, that he'd earned the right to wear it. Conversely, he realized, he hadn't actually worn one for a while.

At the top of the stairs, Calavera knocks on the door.

The man who answers it is small, well-kempt, and shatters the image of the classic put-upon tailor in rolled-up sleeves with a measuring tape perpetually hung around his neck. This tailor is clad in his own perfect buttoned-up double-breasted suit with a flamboyant pocket square of many colors. It somehow matches the mask he wears, a gold, almost silken looking hood with an elaborate pattern of measuring tapes looping in every direction like streamers during a parade.

"You don't have an appointment," the Tailor dryly informs him.

No one knows the old man's real name.

He was always simply been "The Tailor."

"No," Calavera admits.

At that moment Victor steps around his arch-nemesis.

There's no change in The Tailor's expression.

"Neither do you," he informs Vic in the same neutral tone.

"We're very sorry to inconvenience you, Señor Sastre," Victor apologizes with a respectful bow of his masked head.

"*You* may be sorry," Cal corrects him.

Calavera's entire posture and demeanor have switched in the short walk up that flight of stairs to The Tailor's domain. Victor doesn't realize it, but his old rival has gone into "interrogation" mode, his only real outlet for aggression since leaving wrestling and his villainous life behind.

"We're here to ask about a recent client of yours," Cal tells him, pushing past the smaller man into the shop, pacing straight through the waiting room into The Tailor's private workspace.

Victor sees the old man's entire body stiffen at the gross intrusion.

The Tailor follows him briskly into the fitting area, Victor on his heels.

"I do not divulge information about any of my clients," the Tailor says. "Not even measurements. As you well know, *Señor Calavera*." He oozes the name like it leaves a bad taste in his mouth.

Cal turns to him, stepping close and looming large and menacing. "You may not have noticed, Tailor, but times have changed."

The Tailor looks up into his masked face, unmoved.

"For some, perhaps."

"The museum was just robbed. I'm thinking enmascarados were involved," he barks out authoritatively, shrugging of the confused look Victor is giving his posturing. "Have you fitted any henchmen for a job recently? Or maybe someone looking to splurge some recently acquired disposable income?"

"Very possible," the Tailor admits. "A new suit is not only critical for *field work*, it is the ultimate sign of attainment, after all. Particularly one of mine."

"But did the men...people...we're looking for *attain* suits here?" Calavera asks with more weight behind his voice.

The Tailor only shrugs. "As I said, discretion built this establishment as much as these old hands of mine."

"Señor Sastre," Victor begins respectfully, "My family has always respected the confidentiality of this place. However, there's...more on the line than stolen artifacts from a museum. We need to find these men."

"*We*," the Tailor repeats, and it's unclear whether he's amused or impressed. "That the two of you are seeking such criminals together surely must mean it's a task with many facets. Be that as it may, I cannot betray the trust of my clients. Any clients."

Calavera sighs, exaggerating the gesture, almost theatrically.

"A true sartorial priest," he says.

A headless, armless mannequin form stands at the center of a trifold of tall mirrors. The form is wearing a perfect, classic rendition of a double-breasted pinstriped suit. Probably bullet and fire proof. Its buttons are pure gold, each engraved with a finely detailed Mexican emblem.

Calavera walks over to the newly finished suit. "You haven't lost a step, Tailor. I will say that for you. This is impeccable."

"Thank you," the Tailor says, almost cautiously.

Cal reaches inside his jacket, removing a long, slender glass vial. It has a screw-on cap that is carved in the shape of one of Cal's signature skulls.

It's filled with an iridescent green liquid.

Victor's tone is a deadly warning: "Calavera."

"What did you say once in one of those stupid newspaper interviews you liked to give after you ruined one of my plans?" Cal asks him. "'The truth is a fire?' Something like that?"

Cal unscrews the skull-shaped cap on the vial.

He tips it, letting one drop of the liquid escape and hit the floor beside the mannequin.

It sears the old wood plank like acid.

Exactly like acid.

"That seems a very silly thing to carry around in your suit," the Tailor comments.

"I brought it specifically for this occasion." Cal replies, happy with himself, then suddenly changes tone. "Who's been in this past week, Tailor?" Cal asks. "Anybody flush with cash? Anybody looking to pay you with stolen relics? That wouldn't be a first for you, would it?"

"I accept all forms of payment," the Tailor calmly affirms. "Again, as you yourself well know."

"Well then?" Cal demands.

The Tailor stands mute, resolutely.

Cal holds the vial above the shoulders of the Tailor's newest creation on the form.

Victor's eyes widen.

It's as if Calavera is threatening to dissolve the face of the Mona Lisa.

"Last chance," Cal promises the old man.

"My suits are like my children," the Tailor admits. "But my professional discretion is my soul."

"Then it'll be interesting to see which causes you more pain when it's broken," Cal fires back calmly.

He begins carefully tipping over the vial in his hand.

Victor's iron grip on his wrist stops him.

Their eyes lock.

"Let go," Calavera orders him in a lethal whisper.

Victor shakes his head.

Cal tries to jerk his hand away by force. As Victor attempts to wrestle him under control the vial goes sailing from his hand.

The Tailor steps to one side, narrowly avoiding its arc and the now leaking contents.

The vial smashes atop a decorative Mayan rug, immediately burning through the fabric, and then the half-rotted wood of the floor beneath.

Victor's grip relents, and Calavera yanks his arm away.

The two square off, ready to go at it for a third time since Cal's return.

Cal practically breathes into Victor's mouth. "I'll lose my mask before I let you get in my way, especially now. Those days are over. They're *over*."

"You haven't changed," Victor fires back. "Not one pinche bit."

"Victor, your language," Cal taunts him.

"I told Gus this wouldn't work. And it's not even because you're still a villain. It's because you're still a loser. That's always been your problem. That's always been your whole family's problem. *You can't stand being the losers!*"

"¡Te voy a matar!" Calavera growls in his face.

The two suddenly reach for each other, both grasping the back of the other man's neck with one hand while the other hand reaches for the opponent's elbow. They've "locked up" this way thousands of times in the past, it's the standard way of starting a pro-wrestling match, and it's always led to the most spectacular violence of both their lives.

"Gentlemen!" the Tailor shouts unexpectedly.

Vic and Cal both pause, still grasping each other.

"Intimidation is one thing," the old man says, his tone returning to normal as he stomps out his smoldering rug. "But I will not tolerate violence on these premises. I haven't in the fifty years I've been in business, and I won't have that streak broken by you two. Is that clear?"

It's suddenly like being chastised by both of their grandfathers, and the history and tradition and authority implied in that association is more than enough to take the starch out of their tempers.

At that moment they both realize if they're not going to fight then they're really just hugging each other. Both men relinquish their holds and step back awkwardly, clearing their throats.

Victor points at him seriously. "I told Bustamante this was a joke waiting to become a disaster. And it's over. I'm done. The FBI wants you here, fine. But if you're still here after they catch these thieves then I'm coming for you. And this time we'll finish it. The loser *won't* leave town."

Before Cal can respond Victor turns and storms out of the shop.

"I still want the information, Tailor," Calavera says to the Tailor after Vic is gone. "And the técnico isn't here to baby-sit you anymore."

The Tailor sighs.

"Very well. I'll tell you what you wish to know. However, I will do so with the understanding you will never be fitted in this shop again. You forfeit your right and ability to patronize this establishment."

Those words actually pierce Calavera's frightening interrogator's demeanor.

He pauses. He looks down at the suit he's currently wearing, unconsciously stroking the stitch work.

Cal glances around the ancient, ramshackle shop nevertheless filled with sartorial wonders.

He looks back at the Tailor.

"Well then," he says. "I'll just have to make do with the stunning wardrobe I have now, hidden compartments and custom armoring or no."

The Tailor sighs. "Very well. I did fit some rather large and put together gentlemen before the robbery. Premium extras, too, much like you used to order..."

Cal gives a self-affirming nod at the admission, but before he can follow up, The Tailor interrupts.

"And...this frail...*man*...wrapped from head to toe in quite foul-smell-ing bandages."

Calavera blinks.

"You're kidding me."

The Tailor shakes his head.

"Any idea where he...*it*...is now?"

Reluctantly, the Tailor nods.

FATHERLY ADVICE

The Victor Estate stands on a well-appointed street in Tropico Heights, Rencor's old-money suburb. Its wealthy homes are walled-in for security just outside of town with the open desert as everyone's backyard.

Victor's grandfather bought the mansion in the late 50's for a price that makes Victor ache whenever he thinks about it. It wouldn't purchase a corner of a condo downtown at today's rates.

Victor II meets his son at the front entrance of the house, a door of stained glass forming the profile of the family's iconic mask. Marble columns in the shapes of "V's" surround it. He's dressed down for the evening in a satin robe and monogram slippers.

"Come in, mijo," his father bids him. "It's good to see you around here. You don't make it out often enough anymore."

"Is Grandpa awake?" Victor asks.

"No. And even if he was, he doesn't come down stairs unless he has to. He still won't use the electric chair or the elevator we put in. It takes him a whole afternoon to climb up or down the steps."

They walk down the Hall of Victory, a long, broad corridor lined with trophy cases and shelves containing the higher-end in-ring and crime-fighting mementos from over sixty years of El Victor exploits. At this point, much like the lower-end stuff he's been parting with lately, no one can remember whether many of the artifacts are genuine, or whether they're simply movie props. Grandpa Victor would have everyone believe he warded off real vampires in the mountains of Michoacán with the ornate Aztec totem hovering in its own Lucite display case. Victor II insists the same piece is cheap roadside junk that's only valuable because he carried it in his seminal film *EL VICTOR VS. EL VAMPIRO AZTECA.*

The youngest Victor pauses briefly beside an expansive, framed, and professionally lit American-market one-sheet of *EL VICTOR AND RAH'S MUMMY ASSASSIN,* illustrated with a tableau of his father being pursued by the mummy in question, a towering figure of menace and mysticism.

"You okay, mijo?" his father asks.

"Yeah. I just...did you ever see a real one of these things?" he asks, tapping the glass frame of the poster over the image of the mummy.

Victor II shakes his head. "It was just some mongoloid from down south in a costume, like always. I never saw a real mummy. Who has?"

"I did!" Grandpa Victor's withered voice cries down from beyond the hallway and above the staircase beyond, in defiance.

Victor II sighs. "No, Papa, you didn't!" he calls back.

"Yes I did!" the ancient enmascarado insists. "I unraveled him by hand! That's how we did it back then! You kids don't know anything!"

"Go back to bed, Papá!" Victor II bids him.

Grandpa Victor's "goodnight" is just a guttural sound of general frustration and reprimand.

Victor II leads his son to the kitchen, where he pours them both coffees as they sit around an oak table.

"Make yourself at home, mijo."

Victor reaches up and scratches absently around the laces of his hood. "I almost forget how to feel at home like this."

"Here, or anywhere?"

"Anywhere. I guess."

Victor II sighs. "It's harder on you than it was on me, or your grandfather. The business was different then. The fans were different. You have to spend more time in the hood, earning every dollar, every fan. I blame the internet."

"The internet helps, Papá. You just have to know how to *work* it. It's like a crowd that way."

Victor II shrugs. "I'm an old man. I'm allowed to blame it."

"Can I ask you something? It's something I never really...thought to ask before. I guess because it didn't matter, or at least I thought it didn't."

"What's that, mijo?"

"Do you...*hate* the Calaveras? Did you really hate Calavera II, and... do you still?"

His father's heavy, scarred brow dips. "Such a question. Why ask it now?"

Victor shrugs, realizing with some relief the family must have missed the news all day.

"Well," his father begins with a sigh of contemplation, "there were certainly times I did. But there are times you think you hate everyone, even the people you love. Not to say I loved the bastard. Not at all. But after years of fighting each other it becomes...I don't know...almost a partnership. When you know your enemy as well as you know your own family all of those feelings get mixed up. And you start to know how much you depend on each other. Your livelihoods, even who you are, it all depends on each other, on the battle."

"The whole 'good can't exist without evil' thing?" Victor asks wryly.

His father laughs. "Mijo, it's only about good versus evil for the fans. For us it's about winning and losing. And you can't win unless you have an opponent. Even if you do, if no one cares about them, then winning won't matter. The Calaveras are good opponents. They always were. That's why...I can't hate them."

"Would you ever team up with one of them, though?"

The older man's jovial expression with all its homespun wisdom suddenly evaporates.

"In Hell I would!" he shouts. "That hijo de puta broke my jaw, my back, my skull! He tried to blow up this house *three* times!"

"All right, Papá. All right. Calm down."

"Are you thinking about the past, mijo?"

Victor shakes his head. "I'm thinking about the future."

"The future will come no matter how much you worry about it, you know."

"I know," Victor says, and his eyes are perhaps the hardest his father has ever seen them at that moment. "But I want to be ready for it."

• • • •

At that same moment on the opposite side of Rencor, a different figure stares at another copy of the movie poster to *EL VICTOR AND RAH'S MUMMY ASSASSIN*. This one like countless others was pasted to the wall of the long-abandoned Peliculas Rencor movie studio decades ago, when the converted warehouse was a veritable factory churning out dozens of films a year.

Surrounded mostly by industrial lots, few have noticed, never mind raised an eyebrow at, all the new activity inside the studio complex. Lights on at all hours of the night. Trucks coming and going. Ancient looking props from what has to be some period-set film being unloaded. Men in haz-mat suits and other costumes. Must be stuntmen, right?

The figure tilts its head a bit, then a gaunt, nigh-skeletal finger wrapped in dusty bandages feebly tugs at a lose corner of the poster, trying to pull it off the wall. But the relic is one with the old paint and concrete by now.

Giving up, the figure just stares at the garish illustration of the film's monster, almost like looking in a mirror.

HOME INVASION

Stella and Calavera's rental car pulls up outside Gimnasio Victoria just after midnight.

The nondescript brick building appears totally dark.

"Now," Stella proclaims, "march your ass in there, make up with the big dumb do-gooder, and let's put this case away and get out of this damn town."

"You know, you were sexy until you started acting like my mother," Cal says, sullen.

"I can't even imagine what you put such a woman through, and I don't want to. What I do know is we were ordered to work with local PD on this case. Local PD has assigned Victor. So you are *going* to work with Victor. I have one job in the Bureau right now, Cal, and it's making sure you do what they order you to do. I can't afford to blow that very simple task."

They've had this argument for most of the evening, ever since Calavera returned to the hotel without Victor and Stella pried out of him what happened at the Tailor's shop. When they began going back and forth, Calavera was adamant he'd never work with the técnico again, not under any circumstance. It took Stella exactly three hours and twenty-three minutes to move him off of that, and another two hours to wear him down on coming here.

Neither of them has ever been more exhausted.

"You owe me," Calavera tells her, buttoning his jacket and opening his door.

"No, I don't. Do your job."

Cal exits the vehicle.

The door to the lobby isn't kept locked, as the mailboxes are installed there, but the door beyond that one is. It appears no one's home, at least on the gym level. Cal searches for some type of buzzer or call button for the floors above, but finds none.

Peering over his shoulder to make sure Stella can't see him inside the antechamber, Calavera removes a universal lock pick from one of his pockets. He sticks the digital device in the door's keyhole and waits. A second later it beeps and he turns it like a key, unlocking the door and letting himself in.

He takes in the once familiar hybrid smell of sweat and Tiger Balm, not realizing how much he actually missed it. Making sure he is indeed alone, the intruder cautiously strolls past the MMA octagon with an eye-rolled 'tsk' then the two lucha rings. He absent-mindedly runs a hand along the canvas surface of a ring apron, then up to the bottom rope. He stops for too long a moment, clutching the steel cable wrapped in years worth of cloth tape, then withdraws his hand with a sigh.

"Gimnasio Victoria..." he muses to himself. It's not the first time he's been here, of course. The gym factored into several of his dastardly schemes back in the day. He even infiltrated the place once posing as a student, unmasked but in heavy prosthetic facial disguise (he's never even told his father about that one. The old man would've brained him).

Then it occurs to him, the mail boxes...*box-es*...other addresses? Other offices? Other levels? He tries to recall the height of the exterior compared to the height of the ceiling above him and it hits him all at once.

"...got to be fucking kidding me..." he chastises himself.

It takes him less than five minutes to locate the 'secret' elevator. With true super villains in shorter and shorter supply, Victor appears to have gotten very sloppy. Not enough challenges keeping him on his toes, Cal thinks to himself, spotting the nearly century-old key-operated lock. He makes shorter work of that than he did the entrance, thinking to himself "this is for you abuelo" as it pops open.

Calavera steps off the elevator a few moments later, and suddenly finds himself in Victor's living space.

He tried for years during their feud to locate the fabled Victor secret headquarters, just as three generations of Victors had attempted to find and infiltrate the Calaveras' lair. Neither family had ever scored that coup.

"It was here the whole damn time," Calavera mutters under his breath. "Right above the gym. Never thought even *he'd* be that obvious. I can't believe..."

He trails off, shaking his head. Still and all, finally invading Victor's home is helping Cal recover a piece of his dignity right now.

He walks amongst what currently appears to be more of a storage unit than a living room, eyeing all the carefully bubble-wrapped mementos and props. Cal recognizes the one-man submersible pod he designed himself to break into a waterfront art gallery, half-crated against a wall of Victor's loft.

"Hijo de p—...this is mine!" he breathes venomously. "How did he... it's *mine*! I built *that* too!" he hisses, jumping from one trophy piece to the next. A half-dismantled ray-gun here, a creature in a tank there. "That's MY Mer-Monkey!!!"

Calavera looks around, eyes frantically scanning for some source to unleash the sudden torrent of rage he feels.

There's still no one in sight.

He looks from artifact to artifact, his gaze finally resting on the encased chupacabra robot.

Calavera removes the vial of acid with which he threatened The Tailor and pops the door open. He stares at the shoddy movie prop, bringing the vial in his hand an inch from frayed fur, preparing to thumb the cap open and drip its destructive contents.

Part of him, in a voice that sounds very much like his father, is screaming for him to torch the piece of memorabilia.

Another part, in a voice that sounds like Stella's, reminds him that's not what he came here for, none of this is.

The decision is made for him in the form a small, steel-hard foot kicking him in the wrist, knocking the vial from his ringing hand. It lands on the floor without shattering.

"¡Coño!" he curses at the sudden pain.

Calavera turns to find he's been assaulted by a dark-haired young woman half his size who is currently poised in a kickboxing stance within striking distance of him.

Gypsy's eyes suddenly soften, then light up. "Oh-my-god! You're El Mil Calaveras the Third!"

Caught off-guard by this whole bizarre turn of events, Cal just nods.

"I am *such* a fan of your matches with Victor! You have no idea!"

And with that, Gypsy springs into motion and kicks Calavera fiercely between his legs.

All of the air in his body seems to exit at once, and Cal finds himself involuntarily slumping to his knees.

The surprise is almost worse than the pain, but the pain is absolutely more paralyzing.

He stares up at her with wide eyes, unable to even find the words.

"I'm really *sorry* about this," Gypsy apologizes sincerely, preparing to sidekick him right in the head.

"Freeze! FBI!" a new voice commands her.

Both Gypsy and Calavera turn their heads to see Stella holding her service pistol on them.

"Oh, good!" Gypsy waves at her excitedly. "I got him! It's Calavera!"

"I know who he is, you fruitcake!" Stella shouts back at her. "I'm talking to you. Put your hands above your head."

"But I—"

"Now!"

Gypsy obeys, frowning.

At her feet, Calavera stands with a painful groan.

"Do me a favor," he says to Stella. "Shoot her."

"Why?" Stella asks. "I'm already her biggest fan."

"What's going on here?" Victor demands.

He's standing just outside the private elevator, staring at them wide-eyed in anger and confusion.

Stella quickly holsters her weapon and holds up her hands as if she can physically restrain him from reacting further. "This was a minor misunderstanding."

"*I told you to install that biometric lock!!!* He was going to burn the building down, boss.*" Gypsy insists.

"Oh, I was not," Calavera says, sounding more annoyed than anything else. "It was just a little acid. I was just going to scorch a couple of your ego trophies, if anything."

Stella glares razor-edged daggers at him.

"Get out," Victor instructs them. "Both of you. Now."

"No," Stella says firmly. "Listen, I don't care if the two of you have been rivals since little league or who stole whose girlfriend or whatever the hell it is between you, neither of you are those guys anymore and it doesn't matter."

"Yes, it does," Victor states flatly.

"I agree with him on that," Cal says.

"I mean it doesn't matter to *me*. We're here to do a job. Yours, both of yours, is *supposed* to be catch criminals. Mine is to make sure you do your damn job. I'm ready. Are you?" She looks at Cal. "Do you want to go back to small money somewhere between America and Japan?"

To Victor she says: "Do you want to go back to...whatever it was you did every day before we came to town?"

Calavera stares at the ground, grumbling to himself the whole time like a petulant child.

Victor stares at Stella for several moments, then looks at Gypsy, his eyes asking her opinion.

She offers him a warm, albeit tense smile.

"Well...it'd be more exciting than online auctions, boss..." she says.

Calavera lifts his head and stares at her in confusion for a moment before looking at Victor, aghast.

"You were gonna *sell* my Mer-Monkey?" he utters in a genuinely hurt tone.

His arch-nemesis stares back at him. They can all practically see wheels spinning behind Victor's eyes.

They wait, even Calavera.

"OK!" he finally breaks the silence, nodding at Gypsy. "OK, Agent O'Shaugnessey." Victor gives a mocking half-salute to Stella as he strides right up to Calavera.

"OK. But after we solve this thing," he says to the rudo, who finally stands fully upright, "you're on the next plane...or you're in the ring. Either way, you won't leave Rencor on your feet."

Calavera takes a deep breath, every molecule of his body wanting to rise to that challenge.

Looking at Stella, and the gaze she shoots back at him, is the only thing that stays his hands.

Forcing a smile through his mask, Calavera looks back at Victor.

"All right...But I have one question for you, hero. *Do you believe in living mummies?*"

STUDIO SHOWDOWN

Stakeouts have long been an occupational hazard for both masked hero and masked villain, even if they both use the pursuit for vastly different purposes.

Rarely, however, do you find a hero and villain on the same stakeout, in the same car. In fact, in the history of Rencor it's never happened.

Calavera shifts uncomfortably in the small bucket seat of Victor's two-seater bomber. They're watching the front entrance the old Peliculas Rencor movie studio where many of Victor's family's movies were shot. It's a ghost town now, and the once golden sign painted on the tall pueblo arch under which many B-movie stars once passed daily is faded almost to the point of being illegible.

"I can't believe the Tailor gave it up," Victor marvels, more to himself than Calavera.

"He didn't," Cal states flatly. "He didn't give me the studio, anyway. That would've violated his precious ethics."

"Then...what are we doing here?"

"The Tailor gave me the name on a Chinese take-out carton left behind by one of the goons he fitted. Comida Chi—"

"Comida China y Donuts. *Mom's* Comida China y Donuts." Victor interrupts. "I worked at this studio for years, it was the only catering they could afford towards the end..."

"Yeah? Well, one of *Mom's* bicycle boys delivered food to, and I quote, 'a burn victim' at this address."

"Burn victim?"

"All bandaged up." Cal says, orbiting a twirling finger around his own head.

Victor almost doesn't catch himself before he grins.

Calavera shifts again, agitated.

"So did your girl—"

"You mean the one who nailed you in the huevos?" Victor chuckles back, before turning overly serious. "She's not my girl, she's just my research assistant and—"

"Wait, I thought she was your *personal physician*?" he jibes, complete with air quotes.

"That...too..."

"Uh huh...Well, did she find any clues in all that research she was doing?"

"YES, she did," Vic says, remembering a folder of printouts Gypsy provided him earlier. He cycles through the data and photos, happy to get back to business.

"Hm. The museum curators admitted that most of those amulets from the ransacked cases were actually junk—"

"Yeah, fakes put in place like 15 years ago when the real pieces were stol—" Cal catches himself.

Victor slow burns a look into him like a disappointed parent, but continues. "Yeah. They kept them on display so as not to lose face with the public or pay rising insurance premiums."

"Lying putos."

Vic struggles to contain himself, when a paragraph circled in red sharpie and flanked by hand-written exclamation points catches his eye. "But one of them was possibly legit. Recently unearthed from a construction site downtown. Yeah, I remember that news story..."

"Continue." Cal says, trying to hide his degree of interest.

"Pre-Aztec, pre-Mayan even. It was on display in the Egyptian wing because nobody at the museum knew where else to put it." Victor reads from Gypsy's notes. "Some professor from down south thinks it might be 'a legendary totem imbued with mystical energies?' One of these pictures is supposed to be it but I can't tell them apart."

"Mystical energies? Like weather-controlling shit or ancient 'roids? Great." Cal says sarcastically, with a tinge of legit concern. "You believe any of that?"

"You and I arc on a stake-out together looking for a living mummy. Why get skeptical now?"

"Point." Calavera sighs.

He and Victor, each with half the photos, give them another look, then both frown, shoot each other an almost embarrassed glance, and toss them out opposite windows.

"*Magic amulet...*" they both grunt in unison.

The quiet that follows can't last long enough for Victor and can't be broken quickly enough by Calavera.

"Can I ask you a question?"

"We're stuck in this car together, so you definitely have the ability."

"Yeah, about the car. What is this two-seater convertible thing with you heroes? I like a big sled, luxury...bullet-proof windows, room to move around, load the back seat with henchmen, nice big trunk for—"

"Capes."

"Capes?"

"Yeah. The convertible lets your ring cape flow over the back, when you're chasing someone down. Plus these cars are easy to get in and out of—"

"You never wore a cape out on the street."

"Grandpa did, so did my dad at first. It was a whole thing."

"Yeah, come to think of it, my granddad and dad were the same. Did those guys even own shirts back in the day?"

"Desert gets cold at night." Vic mumbles, raising the zipper on his ring jacket a bit."

Cal notices, and keeps on him.

"Can I ask you another question?"

Victor's sigh isn't enough to stop Cal from rambling on.

"What's with your clothes, carnal? Seriously?"

Victor shoots him a genuinely surprised, instantly offended look.

"What? What does that mean?"

"Every time I've seen you since I've been back you're wearing the same tired, busted ring jacket you were wearing ten — hell, twenty — years ago. And you're not even trying with the rest of this wardrobe. And that same ol' mask design..."

Victor stiffens and his eyes narrow, dangerously. "What about my mask?"

Calavera immediately holds up his hands. "Just an observation." He runs one of those hands over his own sparkling-new hood with its brilliant colors. "New gear can make you a new man. Add some flames, Vic, or Aztec stuff or at least some barbed wire around the V or...something."

"You look like a clown, flames and skulls and leopard print and zebra stripes...it's like someone melted the hood from a lowrider over your head" is all Victor says. "Besides...changing your máscara disrespects the generations before you."

"You know what I think?"

. . . .

"I think I'm in love," Agent O'Shaugnessy moans out with a mouth still half-full of her second chocolate-frosted buttermilk, giving the heavy square mound of fried cake dough a look of genuine affection.

Gypsy, having just witnessed the carnage of Stella tearing apart a grande order of Mom's noodles so fast it never even threatened to cool has lost her own appetite. She instead stares at the silent two-way radio handset like it's a watched kettle that just won't come to a boil, and sighs.

"This joint is a real dump," the Fed says, gesturing to the fluorescent lights, stained white and red linoleum everywhere and the fogged-up steam tables, "but fuck-yeah 24-hour kung-pao and bear claws. You gonna finish that?"

Gypsy considers how difficult it was to pull her jeans over her ass this morning and surrenders her strawberry-stuffed cruller, a mere two bites in.

"Are stakeouts always this boring?" Gypsy asks the experienced field agent, trying to find something to talk about.

"Usually. And they go on for days and weeks too. Although with our two masked friends, things seem to accelerate at unusual speed."

"Between their two careers, no one knows the criminal landscape of this city better than them. You watch." Gypsy perks up.

"You're a real...what was the word Cal used the other day...'mark' for this Victor huh?" Stella says, instantly regretting it when she's answered by the combination of insulted and hurt look on Gypsy's face.

"Sorry, I'm new. What I meant was, you have a wicked impressive array of degrees and background, you could write your own ticket anywhere. And...you really don't want to talk about this." Stella gives up, noticing Gypsy staring at the still silent radio again.

"About as much as you want to talk about what trouble you got in with the Bureau to get stuck babysitting El Mil Calaveras."

"Touché." Stella grunts out, sucking the last molecules of strawberry glaze off her fingers.

Gypsy can take no more. "I think we should head back over to the studio!"

"We're back-up. Back-up keeps its distance."

"I think they're in trouble..."

"They're not in trouble. From what I've seen, these two can take care of themselves. Relax."

"I think...What if they're trying to kill each other...again?" Gypsy asks soberly.

The frightening realization hits Stella at the same moment. She grabs the radio

"You know what I think?"

. . . .

"No, I don't know *what you think*..." Victor spits back at Calavera in an increasingly raised voice that threatens to give away their hiding spot, were anyone else around.

Calavera's voice is starting to crack a bit from talking so much. "Well, I think I left this city and it forced me to evolve, and you stayed behind and remained exactly the same. And it hasn't served you well."

"Maybe I don't need to overcompensate with a thousand masks and as many suits. I didn't lose."

"You didn't lose our last match. But trust me, Victor, from what I can see you definitely *lost*."

"You know, back in the day, when you used to have me trapped or tied to a chair somewhere, I thought your stupid monologues and manifestos were just about the worst torture you could inflict. But you psycho-analyzing me? Way worse. *Way* worse."

"Because I'm right?"

Victor just grunts.

"All I'm saying—"

"Shut up!" Victor instructs him.

"If you don't want to hear the truth—"

"No, shut up and look!"

Victor points. Across the street, a beaten van turns off the street in front of the studio and glides through the disused front entrance.

"Let's go, hero," Calavera bids him, opening his door without waiting for an answer.

Victor frowns, but nods.

They both exit the car and Victor walks around the hood to join Cal.

They both forget their two-way radios.

The duo creeps across the street and stealthily enters the studio, sticking to the many shadows of the allegedly abandoned, deserted ruin.

Up ahead they see the van drive past the old domed sound stage and stop in front of large, boxy aluminum warehouse at the end of the complex.

A massive enmascarado in one of The Tailor's suits and a simple yellow and black hood climbs out of the van. He's wearing a large red fez hat with black tassel on top of his mask. Tattoos are visible on his neck and wrists.

"That's a henchman if I ever saw one," Calavera says. "And I've recruited my share."

"I have the scars to prove it."

Cal laughs. "Yeah, that escaped mental patient with the axe clipped you a real good one that time, didn't he?"

Victor glowers at him.

"So, how do you want to play this, hero? Call for backup? You're not quite officially working for Bustamante, remember?"

"A Victor doesn't call the police until the bad guys are tied back-to-back and unconscious."

"I could've done without the motto, but I like the spirit."

"I'll tell you what, Calavera," Victor says, "since nothing about this makes sense, let's go with it. You want to see change? You take the front. Go straight in. Like a hero. *I'll* sneak around back."

"Like the villain?"

"Like...a sneakier hero."

Calavera grins. "You've intrigued me. Let's do it."

"What are the odds you screw me on this?" Victor asks him.

Cal chuckles. "I can't tell whether or not you're joking."

"I'm not."

"Yeah. Not your strong suit. I'd say about seventy percent. Vast improvement over the old days, que no?"

Victor can't argue with that.

They part ways in the middle of the studio, Victor taking the long way around the building and disappearing into the shadows.

Watching him go, Calavera creeps up alongside the van, which is parked by the open bay doors of the warehouse.

"We want our money and we want it now!" a gruff, vaguely familiar voice demands.

It's 88, the Otomies mouthpiece from the alley in Li'l Zee. His two favorite gang thugs join him (Cal recognizes the bruises and cuts he gave them both). 88 himself has one arm cast up all the way to the shoulder.

He's talking to the high back of a vintage leather chair faced away from the doors. Its unseen occupant is hunched over a card table, which Calavera can make out is covered with dusty Egyptian artifacts from the museum heist.

"Your money is coming," a raspy voice belonging to the chair's occupant assures the bangers.

"No, cabrón, *now!*" 88 demands. "This was supposed to be in-and-out shit. We were just hired to drive that truck into the place and help your boys grab whatever we could carry. The dude who hired us never said anything about having to get our money from some freak. Now those other two luchadores are involved, it's all over Instagram and shit. If the cartel finds out we're freelancing they'll hang our families' guts on hooks from a bridge."

"I told you," the raspy voice reiterates, "it's coming. Do not doubt our master..."

The owner of the voice stands up from the chair.

Having climbed through a back window, Victor is in position to see it, and he is awe-struck. Beyond that, however, rising steadily and heatedly from within him is also a spark of elation.

It's the mummy.

He's real, and he's standing there conducting an evil plot.

For Victor it's the moment of a lifetime.

The mummy's entire head and face are bandaged save for dark hollows over the eyes and mouth. The filthy rags stand in sharp contrast to the perfect chairman-of-the-board suit The Tailor made for him.

Calavera, still watching from his own vantage point, feels none of the awe Victor experienced. He feels a sense of professional betrayal. This is still *his* city. This is the type of crime of which *he* was once regarded as the undisputed master.

And this bandaged...*thing*...is impinging on his legacy.

Composing himself, he lights a cigar and walks out of the shadows, slipping a casual demeanor on like one of his finest suits.

"Buenas noches, mi amigos," he greets them warmly. "Nice night for an evil plot to go tits up on you, eh?"

"¡Chingón!" 88 practically screeches. He and the other two Otomies draw automatic pistols from their pants.

"Wait!" the mummy commands them, his rasp becoming a hiss.

"We're going to blast this fool!" 88 insists.

"NO! This...is not the masked man we were expecting. You'll do as you're told as long as I'm holding your money!" the Mummy says.

Calavera folds his hands in front of him, cigar perched between his fingers. "He's got a point there, mijo."

"Shut up, old man!"

"Lower your weapons!" the Mummy orders them again.

88 hesitates, but eventually obeys, and his thugs follow suit.

"So, I couldn't help but overhear there's an unseen mastermind in this mix here," Calavera continues. "That's an exciting twist. It's classic, like this place. Whoever is pulling the strings on all of you; he's obviously my kind of rudo."

"And he would concur, *Señor Calaveras*," the mummy wheezes in reply, with a respectful bow of the head. "Your timing is as impeccable as your wardrobe, and your reputation precedes you. We hoped you'd find us before we had to find you."

Calavera is slightly taken aback. "So this," he gestures to the studio around them, "was all a trap to lure in Victor. Then what? He becomes the bait for me? Cut to the chase, what's the long game here?"

"Join us in our...forthcoming venture...and the master will give you all the details himself."

"I *knew* it!" Victor cries out from the shadows, breaking through them in a moment of rage and abandon. "I knew this was a double-cross right from the start!"

Charging forward in both anger and excitement, Victor never sees the masked rudo in the fez rush up on an interception course. He also doesn't see the butt of the pistol that collides with his skull a moment after that. Victor hits the floor hard, the momentum of his broken sprint causing him to slide several feet across it before he halts with a groan.

"My new retainer," the mummy informs Calavera.

Cal sighs, pinching the bridge of his nose through his mask and shaking his head.

The fez-wearing goon stands triumphantly over the fallen técnico, gun trained on him.

No mask could hide the deep frown on Calavera's face.

"So then," the mummy says to him, "El Mil Calaveras...how would you like to be free of your government leash? We can make that happen for you. If you're willing to embrace what you *were* and cast off what you claim to have become."

"I'm almost sorry, Victor," Calavera says to the fallen hero in a tight voiced tone unfamiliar even to him. "Almost."

"Don't worry about it," Victor manages after a moment, lifting his battered head from the floor. "I figured us trying to tag team would end this way."

Cal looks to the mummy, and sighs in frustration.

"Me for him," he says simply. "That's my deal."

The hollows in the mummy's bandages that pass for eyes stretch wide. "You would barter for the life of a técnico? More than that, your most hated enemy? The man who banished you from your home?"

"Hm. For a resurrected ancient mummy you sure know your local lucha history. I'm bartering for this idiota's life. Yes. If I wanted him dead I could have killed him a thousand times myself. But that's not what our fight is about. You..." he says pacing toward the creature, gesturing a finger like a school teacher giving a lecture, "You don't know anything about being a villain. You're just a bad guy."

The mummy shakes his head. "Then I have to say...you're not the Calavera I was commanded to bring to the master. He'll be disappointed, but knowing you are both dead and out of his way should be a worthy salve."

No one in the building hears the rental car until it's bursting through the tin outer wall, shattering stacks of rotting crates with a deafening impact.

The Otomies turn their pistols in the direction of the sudden intrusion and begin firing immediately. It doesn't slow the rental car or even cause it to swerve from its course, which ends when all three Otomies are thrown over its hood then to the floor violently, their pistols scattering.

Gypsy and Stella both emerge from the bullet-riddled car, give each other an elated congratulatory glance, then fall on the recovering Otomies.

Stella kicks away 88's pistol before the gang leader can reach for it with his good arm. She extends a telescopic baton and points the blunted end an inch from his face.

"FBI! Act *smahtah* than you look, baldy!" she shouts down at him, her New England accent returning in her excitement.

On the other side of the car, Gypsy delivers a stiff Muay Thai kick to the side of one of the Otomies' heads as the punk recovers on his knees, knocking him unconscious. The third banger manages to retrieve his gun only to have it kicked from his hand, after which Gypsy grabs his head by his hair and pulls it down into her knee, smashing his face. In the same fluid motion she breaks into a pure lucha libre move, leaping up and wrapping her legs around his head before arching backwards and flipping him with a perfect Huricanrana.

"Do something, you fool!" the mummy screams at the Fez, somewhat out of character and with a fuller, more frantic and perhaps Latin accented voice.

He then gathers two armfuls of amulets from the table and bolts towards the van, while his thug panics in the anarchy going on around him, not knowing where to strike first.

Victor takes advantage of the distraction to spring up from his knees, slapping away the fez-wearing rudo's gun and elbowing him in the jaw. Stunned, the henchman throws several skilled punches at him in quick succession. Victor covers up, avoiding any serious damage as he waits for his moment, then ducks under the big man's arms and grabs him around the waist, hoisting him into the air with a fierce groan of effort and slamming him down to the concrete.

"NO—" The mummy's lament never quite reaches an exclamation point as Calavera spears him like an MVP linebacker.

Cal expects to shatter a thousand-year-old corpse into a million pieces or a cloud of dust. Instead he tackles solid, obviously warm flesh beneath the bandages — a man, not a resurrected corpse.

They wrestle for position as amulets scatter everywhere, with the mummy showing a surprising adeptness for grappling. A frustrated and confused Cal finally recalls his glory days in the ring, targets the gaps in the villain's bandaged face and hits home with a two-fingered eye-poke.

Cal for a split second forgets where he is and what year it is, instinctively looking around to make sure a referee that isn't there didn't catch him breaking the rules. The screaming mummy scurries away, clutching his eyes with one unraveling hand and feeling around the floor for amulets with the other.

Calavera gets to his feet and brushes himself off as Victor joins him. They give each other a nod, a silent assurance they're both okay, then realize just how weird that was.

They look back to where Gypsy drags the last of the unconscious Otomies into a pile while Stella throws handcuffs on the equally defeated fez. Gypsy takes a look at his sad, sobbing self and in a moment of recognition aggressively knocks the fez from his head and pulls the ill-fitting mask off.

"Recognize this dweeb?" she triumphantly shouts back to her boss.

"The cage fighting pendejo from my gym!" Victor exclaims to Cal. "He was giving my cousin lip. I had to put the boots to him a little."

"Apparently he held a grudge," Calavera says. "Or he was only there in the first place to *case* you."

"Working the whole time, for...*him*." Victor says in an accusing tone, turning to the sorry scene that is the defeated mummy, sprawled on the floor amidst discarded amulets.

He tries one on, pauses, then frantically moves to another, waiting for some result that has yet to manifest.

"Gotta admire a cabrón who works the gimmick right to the very end." Calavera says, shaking his head in disgust. "Back in the day I might have felt threatened by a guy like this."

"Back in the day," Victor retorts, "you would have put him on the payroll."

"Unfortunately for you, I answer to a higher power!" the mummy replies, in a voice much deeper and more powerful than either of the enmascarados were expecting.

The mummy rises to his feet, and suddenly throws his legs wide, his head back towards the heavens and his chest out, revealing a not-quite-Egyptian looking amulet around his neck that is starting to glow with energy.

"¡Ay dios mío!" Gypsy chimes in, awe and concern in her voice. "I think that's the—"

"—*magic amulet?!?!*" the two masked men finish her sentence in unison, wide-eyed at the sight of the mummy growing half a foot in every direction, roaring like a movie monster while golden lightning sparks around him.

"We need a plan—" Cal begins breathlessly, only to find Victor is already rushing headlong at the mummy like the big, dumb hero Cal should've expected him to be.

"*¡Victoria!*" the técnico cries as he launches a series of forearms into the now keg-sized chest of the mummy.

The force of the blows would crush a normal man's sternum, but the thing only laughs a deep, inhuman laugh. He swings an elongated arm, bashing Victor's head awkwardly to one side, knocking him off his feet.

Calavera has no choice but to launch his own attack on the creature solo. He rushes forward, trying to be less direct as he drops to one knee and fires a strike directly at the creature's kneecap, hoping to take out one of his legs.

Instead, the mummy's now giant hand intercepts Cal's fist and grips it like a vice, fracturing two of the rudo's fingers as he drags Calavera back to his feet. Trying futilely to break the mummy's grasp, the next thing Cal feels is the creature's bandaged skull head-butt him between the eyes. The next thing he feels after that is the floor meeting his prone body.

Gypsy, watching from several yards away, is caught between the Heaven of watching her ultimate childhood fantasies come to life in front of her — genuine heroes battling genuine monstrous villains — and the Hell of seeing her employer and mentor being pummeled.

Stella has a much different reaction.

"I've had enough of this wrestling, B-movie bullshit," she growls, raising her service pistol and rapid-firing her entire clip into the mummy's bandaged torso until the weapon's chamber clicks dryly.

The monster stares down at the new holes in its body, then back up at Stella.

He laughs even louder.

"Well...shit," Stella manages, at an utter and complete loss, the knowledge this is all really happening finally hitting her conscious brain.

Victor seizes the moment of distraction and leaps up onto the mummy's back, attempting to secure a headlock on the thing and wrangle him to the ground. One claw-like hand reaches up and grabs Victor by the shoulder, flipping him over to the ground easily, ripping the técnico's vintage ring jacket in the process.

Calavera has only managed to make it up to one knee when the mummy suddenly seizes him with both arms, lifting him up into the air off of his feet. It squeezes Calavera in a rib-crushing bear hug, cutting off the oxygen from his lungs and causing Cal to groan in agony.

Gypsy and Stella rush him, Gypsy trying to fold the mummy's legs with vicious kicks while Stella pummels his spine and kidneys with her baton. Neither effort stops him, but they do succeed in seriously annoying the creature. He lifts one foot, relaxing his grip on Calavera, and launches it into Gypsy's chest, sending her flying into Stella. The two roll like a tumbleweed before collapsing onto each other.

The mummy's bear hug gives just enough for Cal to free his arms, but cinches back tighter than ever around his even more exposed rib cage once the creature feels him struggling. With trembling hands, Calavera manages to slip a pair of his family's famous skull-adorned brass knuckles over the broken fingers of one hand. He drives several punches into the mummy's skull, feeling it dent, but the creature only wrenches its hold on him all the harder.

"Cal!" Victor yells at him from the ground. "You know how to get out of this! You had the same training I did! Use it!"

Holding Victor in the corner of his gaze, Calavera grits his teeth and lets the brass knuckles slip from his fingers. Cupping his hands behind the mummy's head, Cal raises his feet and plants them against the creature's thighs. With all the momentum he can muster, Calavera rocks himself backward, his weight and the leverage forcing the mummy off his feet. Calavera flips the creature forward, the mummy's grip on him broken as the monster goes sailing over him.

It's a beautiful, textbook escape.

The kind the squarest of técnicos would use.

As the mummy springs to his feet he's met by Victor, who, executing this move for the first time in his life, abruptly and viciously launches a kick into the monster's crotch.

Gypsy, still trying to get her breath back, can't decide what shocks her more, watching Victor employ a rudo tactic, or the movie monster's reaction as it doubles over in obvious pain.

"That thing has balls?" Stella says, head turned like a confused dog.

"I know, right?" Gypsy shouts back.

Cal, still convulsing and gasping for breath himself, catches a distinct look in Victor's eyes, aimed directly at him.

He knows exactly what his former arch-nemesis is thinking.

Calavera fights through the pain and charges forward, leaping at the mummy as Victor shoots in and contorts the supposed monster's body into position for his family's patented finishing maneuver. Calavera grasps the bandaged head in mid-air, and as Victor lowers the boom on the mummy with the Victory Spike, Cal simultaneously and perfectly drives the mummy's head into the warehouse floor with his family's own patented Skull Crusher.

It's a perfectly executed, utterly devastating double-team wrestling move.

"Whoah!" Gypsy leaps up like a fan at ringside. In a burst of inspiration she screams "VICTORY CRUSHER!" coining the maneuver with the fervor of a Japanese TV announcer.

"Ho-lee-shit..." is all an exasperated, although no less delighted, Stella can muster.

Vic and Cal spring to their feet, standing over the mummy's now motionless form, trying to catch their breath. Forgetting who either is, they give each other appreciative slaps to the chest, elated.

Until Stella interrupts, with her baton.

Grumbling something to the effect of being *really* sick of this shit, she golf swings the amulet off the chest of the fallen mummy, sending it several yards past the open bay door into the parking lot.

"Nice swing girl!" Gypsy cheers, pulling up the rear. She inserts herself between the enmascarados, giving them a frustrated look and gesturing down to their foe in a plea to focus on unfinished business.

The mummy, now seemingly shrunken back to his former mass, if not somewhat smaller, lies face up in a quickly expanding pool of red.

"Wait," Cal says. "When did mummies start bleeding?"

"They don't," Victor insists, joining him in inspecting the broken creature.

Gypsy follows, reaching into her pocket and removing a pair of surgical gloves, snapping them over her hands, one and then the other.

Stella watches her, almost dumbfounded, then she reaches in her own pocket and removes her own pair of gloves, doing exactly the same thing.

Carefully, Gypsy begins probing around the bandages of the mummy's face, finally prying several strands away entirely.

The face beneath is not that of a rotted corpse.

"Mummy fake-out!" Cal announces. "I knew it..."

But Victor isn't celebrating.

"Oh my god," Gypsy gasps, hands covering her mouth.

"What?" Stella asks, confused. "Who is it?"

"It's Hernán," Victor says, his voice hollow. "My cousin."

"Lágrima Rojo?" Calavera asks, less moved. "I've never seen the kid unmasked. Better looking than I would've—"

"Cal!" Stella hisses, quieting him.

Victor looks at Gypsy almost helplessly.

"I'm so sorry, boss," she says. "Why would he do this?"

Victor stares back down at the vacant face of Hernán, still scarcely able to process it.

"He...times had been hard on him. He talked about some new job..."

"They got to him," Cal says, more seriously. "Whoever 'The Master' and his people are, *they* got to him. I've seen it before. They offered him a deal that seemed like a dream come true. Then they made him a believer. I heard it in his voice, even disguised like it was."

"Who are *they*? Who is this maestro?" Victor demands.

"I don't know," Cal answers, sincerely. "But I'm very interested to meet whoever it is."

"Why?" Victor asks. "So you can congratulate him?"

"No," Calavera says with a sudden, heady weight to his voice. "So I can put him away."

Both Victor and Stella stare at him in surprise.

Slowly, a grin spreads across Stella's lips.

Victor's expression is still dark, but he's suddenly looking at Calavera in a way he never has before, even if there's more than enough confusion and doubt laced in that gaze.

Slowly, Victor pulls off what's left of his old ring jacket, and lays it across Hernan's head and shoulders.

In the moment, none of them notice the slender figure limping away from the parking lot...

SUNRISE

"Was that real?" Stella asks Cal. "I mean, *obviously* it *happened*. I saw it happen. But was it...real? Does that question even make sense? Jesus, listen to me."

The four of them wait in the studio parking lot in the grey and blue predawn of the morning. Gypsy is half-asleep on Victor's shoulder as the two of them lean on the fender of his car. He comforts her with one arm, cradling the other against his body, fairly sure the shoulder is dislocated.

Stella stands near the bumper with Calavera, who is calmly enjoying the butt of a cigar held between taped-together fingers. Their living suspects, the Otomies and the mummy's henchman, are lined up against the studio wall where she can keep an eye on them, sitting crossed-legged with their wrists cuffed and zip-tied behind their backs.

Stella is trying her best not to shake from sheer nerves. Calavera has yet to see her so rattled by anything. She's never once shaken under fire since being assigned to him. But what she's just experienced wasn't simply gunfire, it was another world intruding on her otherwise normal one.

"It was as real as anything we've ever seen," Cal assures her through his usual din of smoke.

Stella just shakes her head. "Jesus," she repeats, less like a prayer and more like a curse.

She rubs her own elbows, not quite hugging herself.

Cal watches. "Stella...look, I'd hug you, but I'm pretty sure you'd clock me."

"You're goddamn right I would," she snaps back, snorting something like a laugh through her nose. "But...thanks."

"Gypsy." Victor gently nudges his personal physician awake. "Look at that."

Gypsy blinks the half-sleep away and the rest of them fall silent as, above the studio and the city beyond, the sun begins to break on the horizon, lighting everything in sight on fire made of gold and amber.

They hear the sirens as the sun rises in full over Rencor. The first squad car arrives on the scene a moment later. Cal watches Stella step back into the normalcy of dealing with arrests and local law enforcement, and he's grateful she has the distraction. He watches her take charge of the scene, grinning to himself as she barks orders at Rencor PD and begins the process of loading the Otomies into the squad cars.

Stella herself leads the mixed-martial-henchman away, mask and Fez zipped into an evidence bag, until Cal halts her. With a wink, he snatches the evidence bag, as she just rolls her eyes.

Cal walks back and tosses the hat to Victor. "One more for the trophy case," he says.

Before Victor can reply, Cal tosses the mask to Gypsy.

"Here. Your first unmasking trophy" he says to her with a genuine degree of charm and appreciation in his voice. Gypsy holds it like a kid on Christmas morning.

Victor can't help but laugh.

He nods. "Sí. It's yours."

"Well, this has been an experience worthy of a whole new comic book series," Calavera says, "but if I don't hurry I'll miss the continental breakfast at the hotel. So, if you'll excuse me..."

He begins walking casually away.

"¡Oye, rudo!" Victor calls after Calavera, who stops.

"I think I know you a little better than that..."

"What do you mean?" Calavera asks innocently.

"Were you just doing push-ups to get that morning pump in your chest? Because your jacket is a whole lot tighter now."

Stella overhears and makes a b-line for her charge. "Cal..."

Calavera only shrugs. "I'm just a do-gooder thinking about grabbing a celebratory bagel for...doing good, boss."

Stella folds her arms. "Cal, I reloaded my sidearm, if you missed it."

He sighs, unbuttoning his jacket to reveal all of the stolen amulets around his neck.

"Hey!" Gypsy says, the scientist in her protective of the museum's property, but then something occurs to her. "Heeeyyyy...why didn't you grow huge like Hernán did?

"Yeah, that's all we need — you transforming into an even bigger asshole." Stella says, confiscating the amulets and holding them on her baton as if they were venomous snakes. She scrutinizes them with frustration. "Cal! Where's the one...*THE one*...the mummy was wearing?"

"I have no idea," Cal says solemnly, actually a bit miffed himself.

Stella's stare hardens on him.

"I swear on my family's mask, Stella," he says again, more seriously this time.

Stella hesitates, but eventually she nods, accepting that.

"Believe me, I looked," Cal continues. "I already had a spot picked for it back in the family lair, right next to—"

He stops suddenly. "Never mind."

Stella opens her mouth to question him further, but her cell phone rings. She gives Cal a look that says, "We're coming back to this."

Answering the call, Stella suddenly smiles. "Captain Bustamante," she says with genuine enthusiasm, dumping the amulets into another evidence bag, then listens for several moments before replying. "Yeah, you should have seen it...it was actually pretty awesome. I'll tell you all the gory details over dinner, maybe? Oh, hold that thought, I've got another call."

Stella taps the screen of her phone, acknowledging someone barking frantically on the other end before they abruptly hang up.

"The museum brass are on their way, ten kinds of freaked out," she informs them.

"I do *not* like being here for this part," Cal says. "Back in the old days I'd be long gone by now, and it was better that way."

"But in that case I'd be chasing you," Stella reminds him.

"Me too," Victor adds.

"And you wouldn't be happy when we caught you."

At that moment Gypsy's cell phone rings. "Oh hey, it's Captain Bustamante again...*Bueno?*" she answers.

Victor raises his hands questioningly at her.

"Hold on," Gypsy says into the phone, then, to Victor, "He wants me to make sure you don't try to kill Cal."

"Hah!" Calavera explodes. "That should be the other way around."

Stella's phone rings again. "Who?" she says after answering it. "No I do not know who you are Mister *El Barón*? No he isn't free Friday. How the hell did you get this number? What...? Listen, I'm not his secretary."

She ends the call, looking at Cal. "A baron of something wanted to talk to you."

"Damn. Suddenly everybody wants a piece of me."

"Us," Victor corrects him, reading El Barón's caller ID on Gypsy's now-ringing phone. "Hang up on that puto." He commands her.

"Speaking of folks wanting a piece of you..."

Stella points. They all look across the parking lot at a row of long-neglected shrubbery where Cortez and several others carrying various cameras and recording equipment are no longer bothering to hide out.

"Fantastic..." Victor says.

"You're getting better at the sarcasm thing, hero," Cal tells him.

Before Victor can fire back, Gypsy's phone blows up again, and her eyes go wide.

"Umm, boss...it's your pop."

As if on cue, Stella's phone rings yet again, much to her annoyance. She looks at the caller ID, frowning. "1-800-RUDO-RESCUE???"

Both Victor and Calavera's eyes widen.

"Ay, papi," the enmascarados say in unison, probably more fear in their eyes than they displayed during the mummy fight.

"Look," Victor says, "before any of us answer any of these calls or any of Cortez's questions, we need to get a few things straight."

"Like what?" Calavera asks.

"Like, are you planning to stick around?" Victor asks him, almost cautiously.

Calavera cocks his head. "Are you asking me to?"

Victor tenses. "You did save my life."

"And you saved mine. We're even on that score, Victor. This is something else."

Victor looks to Gypsy.

She's smiling ear-to-ear, but she only shrugs, motioning back to Cal.

Calavera looks at Stella.

"It would seem there is *unfinished business* here..." she admits, not so begrudgingly, catching a glimpse of Captain Bustamante's number on her caller list.

"I won't rest until I find whoever did this to Hernán," Victor declares.

"Yeah, and this *Master*...You don't come to my town and try to take down my scores," Calavera adds, then looks to Victor, *"or my rivals."*

Victor locks eyes with Calavera. "I'm not asking you to stay. But I'm not telling you that you can't, either. How's that?"

Before he answers, Calavera reaches inside his jacket and removes one of his stogies. He bites the tip off the end and spits it at the ground before lighting the cigar with one of his matches.

He draws in a mouthful of smoke as he waves the flame of the match into extinction.

Calavera releases the smoke slowly, then grins wide.

Gypsy stifles a giggle.

Stella rolls her eyes.

Calavera looks from both of them to Victor, a dangerous glee filling the eyes behind his skull-themed mask.

"It's a start," he says. "But for now, let's go get some bacon-wrapped hot dogs."

EPILOGUE: MASTERMIND

The Mummy, *the real one*, shambles into the backroom of the Pandemonio from the alley entrance hours after last call.

A small figure cloaked, hooded, and masked all in black awaits him in the shadows.

"Welcome, my friend," its deep voice says to the creature. "I'm pleased the gas from the tanker that reanimated you was so thoroughly effective. It's an experimental compound."

The Mummy raises its thin, decayed arms.

It's holding the lost amulet in the gaunt bandaged-wrapped bones of its hands.

"And you brought me a gift."

Gloved hands reach out and take the object from the Mummy.

"This is only the first piece we need. But don't worry your task is complete, for now."

The cloaked figure inspects the totem, pops of gold lightning still erratically sparking from it, until he delicately trails a finger over one of its inscriptions and the piece seems to deactivate. He draws the dormant totem into his cloak like a loving mother cradling an infant.

"It is a shame about Calavera," the Mastermind laments. "Many strings had to be pulled to convince his new employers to send him back here. Now that he's chosen not to join us, if he stays in Rencor, he'll have to be dealt with. Along with El Victor."

The Mummy performs a gesture akin to a nod, forcing guttural sounds and dust from its mouth.

"I'm so pleased the old days are coming back," the Mastermind says, wracked with a warped version of joy. "Rencor isn't ready."

His new minion has no comment to offer, only further supplication.

"The only question is...who will break first: This city...or its new protectors?"

TO BE CONTINUED?

This book owes its life, in large part, to the ten years I spent as a pro-wrestler. I owe those years to the LIWF Doghouse where I trained to become a worker. I'd like to thank Bobby Lombardi, Laython Wilkerson, Nelson Erazo, Brandon Silvestry, Louie Ramos, and the rest of the Doghouse crew. I can't mention my beginnings as a pro-wrestler without also thanking my mother, Barbara, who believed in me enough to let her son go off as a teen and get the crap beat out of him in a wrestling ring for the rest of his adolescence. I'd also like to thank the amazing luchadores I worked with in and out of the ring over the years who taught me the lucha libre style. El Latino, Chavo Guerrero, Sr., Super Aguilar, and Los Maximos, to name just a few. This book owes the most to Keith Rainville, who first conceived the idea and the story, and rode me to produce my best version of it. We both simply wanted a book and a story like this to exist, and knew it was up to us to make it happen. I love it when a plan comes together.

Matt Wallace

*The publisher wishes to wholeheartedly thank
Christa Faust, Nikki Glowin, Joe Hilliard and Nathan Long
for their time and assistance with this book.*

*I'm also endlessly grateful to my dad for steering young me
to become a Mil Mascaras mark, Dave Hutzley for being
my first customer and paying me in Mexican bootleg toys
instead of dollars, and to giants like Johnny Legend,
Brian Moran, David Wilt and others upon whose shoulders
I have stood since 1996.*

*And finally to Mike Vraney and Eric Caidin...
I hope your ghosts are reading this book
over someone's shoulder.*

MATT WALLACE is the author of *The Next Fix*, *The Failed Cities*, *Slingers* and the *Sin du Jour* series. He's also penned over one hundred short stories, a few of which have won awards and been nominated for others, in addition to writing for film and television. In his youth he traveled the world as a professional wrestler and unarmed combat and self-defense instructor before retiring to write full-time. He now resides in Los Angeles with the love of his life and inspiration for *Sin du Jour*'s resident pastry chef.

WWW.MATT-WALLACE.COM

KEITH J. RAINVILLE is celebrating the 20th Anniversary of his lucha libre pop culture magazine *From Parts Unknown* with the publication of this book. He's also written the reference book *Zombi Mexicano* and the animated feature film *Los Campeones de la Lucha Libre*, designed ring event posters for L.A.'s storied Olympic Auditorium, film credit sequences and opera marketing, while also curating the renowned *Vintage Ninja* website.

WWW.VINTAGENINJA.NET | WWW.FROMPARTSUNKNOWN.COM

JESSE JUSTICE is an All-American, Half-Korean, Eagle Scout, retired Air Force Sergeant, military brat, now living as a mild mannered husband and father in North Carolina. His illustrations have appeared in national TV campaigns and in print and online globally. He also designs wrestling belts, which have to be seen to be believed.

WWW.JESSEJUSTICE.COM

RAFAEL NAVARRO's
LUCHA NOIR

AN OPPONENT CAN DEFEAT YOU, BUT GRAVITY WILL KILL YOU...

A team-based deathsport in an arena built over a wormhole in space is the stage for international conspiracy and global revolution.

5 serialized novellas available at www.Matt-Wallace.com